THE VELVET UND

Copyright © 1997 Omnibus Press (A Division of Book Sales Limited)

Edited by Chris Charlesworth
Cover & Book designed by 4i
Picture research by Nikki Russell

ISBN 0.7119.5596.4
Order No.OP47828

Exclusive Distributors:
Book Sales Limited, 8/9 Frith Street, London W1V 5TZ, UK.
Music Sales Corporation, 257 Park Avenue South, New York, NY 10010, USA.
Music Sales Pty Limited, 120 Rothschild Avenue, Rosebery, NSW 2018, Australia.

To the Music Trade only:
Music Sales Limited, 8/9 Frith Street, London W1V 5TZ, UK.

Photo credits:
Front cover: Gerard Malanga. All other pictures supplied by LFI, Gerard Malanga, Renaud Monfourny & Rex Features. Every effort has been made to trace the copyright holders of the photographs in this book but one or two were unreachable. We would be grateful if the photographers concerned would contact us.

Printed in the United Kingdom by Ebenezer Baylis & Son, Worcester.

A catalogue record for this book is available from the British Library.

NIBUS PRESS
NDON · NEW YORK · SYDNEY

CONTENTS

INTRODUCTION V

ACKNOWLEDGEMENTS IX

THE VELVET UNDERGROUND & NICO 1

WHITE LIGHT/WHITE HEAT 15

THE VELVET UNDERGROUND 25

LOADED 35

LIVE AT MAX'S KANSAS CITY 45

1969: VELVET UNDERGROUND LIVE 49

VU 53

ANOTHER VIEW 61

THE WILDERNESS YEARS 67

SONGS FOR DRELLA 73

LIVE MCMXCIII 81

PEEL SLOWLY AND SEE 87

ANTHOLOGIES 98

INDEX 98

the Velvet Underground
JOHN CALE
LOU REED
STERLING MORRISON
MOE TUCKER
PEEL SLOWLY AND SEE
ALL ACCESS

INTRODUCTION

THE VELVET UNDERGROUND: EXPLODING, PLASTIC, INEVITABLE

They've been called the most influential group of all time; The Beatles aside, it may even be true. Without The Velvet Underground, rock's development would have been a very different story. Their influence on David Bowie is undeniable, and without him glam rock might never have happened. Many people think there would have been no American punk scene without the Velvets (and without that, there'd have been no British one). And you can hear the Velvets' trademarks in virtually every indie guitar band from 1980 onwards. Over eight hundred cover versions of their songs have been recorded, by artists as diverse as June Tabor and Nirvana.

One could strongly argue a case that they were the last of the beats, or the first of the punks; certainly there was nobody else around at the time to touch their intensity (not even The Doors, who look like a melodramatic hippie pantomime in comparison). A good many landmark albums were released in 1967, but it's probable that none have weathered the decades since as well as the Velvets' début. In 1988, readers of *NME* voted 'The Velvet Underground & Nico' the fifth best album of all time.

Considering their subsequent impact, it's amazing that the Velvets' career was so short: just four studio albums, recorded in as many years (none of which even made it into the Top 100). Not until after it was all over did they get much radio airplay. They weren't invited to play at Woodstock. Their first two albums weren't even reviewed by *Rolling Stone*. Their popularity grew largely just by word of mouth. In short, they were not of their time, but ahead of it.

As Mary Harron wrote in *NME*: "The Velvet Underground were the first avant-garde rock band, and the greatest. They were avant-garde in the true sense of exploring uncharted territory. Their songs not only sounded different but they expressed certain feelings, attitudes and kinds of experience that had never been heard in rock music before.

"They took music as far out as it is possible to go without losing consciousness (which is what separates them from their Sixties contemporaries, who did) and made so many new connections – combining poetry with trash, primitiveness with sophistication, delicacy with violence – that they virtually laid the foundations for a new age in rock.

"They would influence later generations, but not their own. During the Velvets' own lifetime, from 1965 to 1970, they were simply notorious as the group who sang about heroin and transvestites and sado-masochism."

That they ran counter to the mainstream was, of course, part of their appeal at the time. As critic Lillian Roxon observed, "the important thing about The Velvet Underground was that in 1966 and 1967 they were as far away as a group could possibly be from the world of incense and peppermints and lollipops and even earnest teenage protest." Nor was this a pose; the Velvets genuinely weren't interested in most aspects of the hippie era, as Lou Reed said at the time: "We had vast objections to the whole San Francisco scene. It's just tedious, a lie and untalented. They can't play and they certainly can't write." Which must have seemed like sacrilege in those days (and was probably why he said it). Much later, he was more specific about what separated the Velvets from their West Coast contemporaries: "It was very funny, until there were a lot of casualties. Then it wasn't funny anymore. That flower-power thing eventually crumbled as a result of drug casualties and the fact that it was a nice idea but not a very realistic one. What we, the Velvets, were talking about... *was* realistic."

Part of their appeal is down to the

sound: deceptively simple, at times sparse and hypnotic, at times abrasive and confrontational. It still sounds like rock; just a different *kind* of rock. But as much as anything else, what lodges in the listener's mind is the subject matter of Lou Reed's lyrics. While most of his contemporaries were attempting to echo and/or imitate both the themes and overall sound of 'Sergeant Pepper', the Velvets' début dealt with the dark and the dangerous: a shady world where hard drugs were the norm and, sexually speaking, you were in the Twilight Zone.

But Reed wasn't just exploiting these subjects for shock value. It was the world he knew. And, as he later put it, "There's a huge amount of compassion, I think, involved in the records. And the compassion is real. A lot of the feelings for outsiders – people from outside the system."

And at least some of the Velvets' long-term intellectual cachet comes from their association with Andy Warhol – a man who was either a great artist or a great con-artist, and probably both. Today, his talent is (still) overshadowed by his image as 'party Andy', a seemingly shallow creature dazzled by celebrity and puzzled by pretty much everything (Gore Vidal once acidly described him as "the only genius with an IQ of 60"). Yet Warhol's uniquely childlike view of the world led him to experiment constantly in his art, and he encouraged that trait in others.

While he may not have known much about music, and had little to do with what the Velvets actually produced, his opinions were certainly taken seriously. And he knew about style, and recognised it in others. Not only did he (undoubtedly) gain The Velvet Underground exposure on a scale undreamed of by most of their contemporaries (even if it backfired on them), he also paired them with Nico for their début – against their wishes, but to their ultimate profit. Would that first album have attracted as many people *without* those wistful ballads, sung in that breathless voice? If only for making them more user-friendly, Warhol's role in The Velvet Underground story should not be underestimated.

And it was his death that instigated the coda to their career, inspiring Reed and Cale to patch up their differences with a masterful tribute to their mentor... which in turn led to the triumphant reunion of The Velvet Underground in the Nineties.

In 1993, Lou Reed summed up their career in retrospect: "Our view of the quality of what we did, I feel... we're in an interesting situation, where we're all alive to see history validate it somehow – not only us, but Andy's faith in us, and our faith in ourselves and the integrity that's gone into it, and all these years never to betray it. We have time to point to as the real judge of who or what did what, first, best and always. The proof is in the work, and the work is on record."

With the passing of Sterling Morrison in 1995, it seems unlikely that The Velvet Underground will ever tour or record again, especially as Reed and Cale seem to be eternally at loggerheads. Meanwhile, we're left with the records examined here - though a slender output, it's one which sounds undimmed thirty years on; and it's certain it will endure for decades to come. As the late Lester Bangs once wrote: "I belong to the generation for whom The Velvet Underground was our Beatles and Dylan combined. I don't care who did feedback first, or if Lou Reed 'sang like Dylan' – modern music begins with the Velvets, and the implications and influence of what they did seem to go on forever. 'Black Angel's Death Song' alone is still ahead of its time, and of course all the other stuff sounds right up to date over a decade later. Who else has created a body of work of which this can be said? The only thing I think would be a mistake in thanking them for this precious gift would be romanticising them too much."

ACKNOWLEDGEMENTS

I'm indebted to the work of those who have travelled this road before me, notably Victor Bockris, M.C. Kostek, Peter Doggett and David Fricke; to William Higham and Patrick Humphries, for letting me raid their respective libraries; to Fred Dellar and Mailan Henning, who intrepidly surfed the net for me; to Glenn Marks, for access to the Glenn Marks Archives and for sharing his own opinions and insight (and for answering my stupid questions); to Chris Charlesworth, for his almost infinite patience; to Neil Gaiman and Alisa Kwitney (the Dreaming Syndicate) for sanity and encouragement; and to Ellie, for being my mirror.

This one's for John Joseph Hogan (1916-1996), wherever he may be.

Peter Hogan, London, 1996

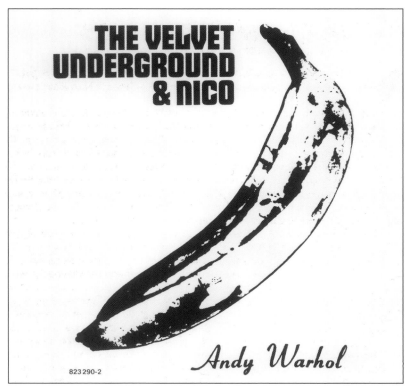

823 290-2

THE VELVET UNDERGROUND & NICO

(VERVE 5008; RELEASED MARCH 1967. CD: VERVE 823 290-2)

Personnel: John Cale (electric viola, bass, piano); Sterling Morrison (rhythm guitar, bass)
Lou Reed (lead guitar, ostrich guitar, vocals); Maureen Tucker (drums); Nico (chanteuse).

In April or June 1966 (accounts differ) Andy Warhol rented the old Scepter Records recording
studio in New York for three nights, at a cost of about $2,000, for The Velvet Underground to
record their first album, which Moe Tucker claims "was recorded, basically, in eight hours. We
pooled our money with Andy, and could afford only eight hours of studio time in New York."
After the group eventually signed to Verve, they were allowed "three more hours at TTG
Studios to clean things up. I think we did 'Heroin' over and repaired the vocals on 'Waiting For
The Man'." Engineers at Scepter were Norman Dolph (who'd also put up some of the money
for the session) and John Licata; in California (John Cale claims the studio was Cameo-
Parkway, not TTG) producer Tom Wilson was assisted by engineer Omi Haden.

According to the classically trained Cale, the band were well prepared for the Scepter session: "We used to tape our rehearsals, to check. Nico was very vulnerable to this. We'd listen and hear her go off-key or hit the wrong pitch at the start. We would sit there and snigger, 'There she goes again !', which might seem a little cruel now. She was deaf in one ear. This made for interesting times. Every now and again she went 'weeergh' and lost control of the pitch; she was very sensitive to all this and when I produced her albums later on I would have her sing and the musicians play in separate sessions. But I mention the playbacks we'd do, because people would say we were just improvising and making a noise on stage, but actually what we did was disciplined and intentioned. Basically, Lou would write these poppy little songs and my job was to slow them down, make them 'slow'n'sexy'. Everything was deeper, too. A song written in E would be played in D. Maureen didn't use cymbals. I had a viola, and Lou had this big drone guitar we called an 'Ostrich' guitar. It made an horrendous noise, and that's the sound on 'All Tomorrow's Parties', for instance. In addition, Lou and Nico both had deep voices. All of this made the record entirely unique."

The Scepter studio was not in the best of condition. Cale: "We went in there and the floorboards were torn up, the walls were out, there were four mikes working. We set up the drums where there was enough floor, turned it all up and went from there." Tucker: "We had a piano at our disposal, so we added some piano parts."

Nominally, the album was produced by Andy Warhol but in reality there *was* no producer - just the two engineers and the band. So, why is Warhol credited? Lou Reed: "The advantage of having Andy Warhol as a producer was that because he was Andy Warhol they left everything in its pure state. They would say, 'Is that okay, Mr Warhol?', and he'd say, 'Oh ... yeah.' And so they didn't *change* any-thing. And so, right at the very beginning we discovered what it was like to be in the studio and record things our way, and have essentially total freedom."

Given the controversial lyrics, this freedom was necessary. Reed: "Andy made a point of trying to make sure that the language remained intact. I think Andy was interested in shocking, in giving people a jolt and not to let them talk us into taking that stuff out in the interest of popularity or easy airplay. He said, 'Oh, you've got to make sure you leave the dirty words in'. He was adamant about that. He didn't want it to be cleaned up and because he was there it wasn't."

All songs were credited to Lou Reed, except 'Black Angel's Death Song' to Reed & Cale, and 'European Son' to all four Velvets.

Warhol's initial idea had been to get a manufacturing and distribution deal and market the record himself. But in 1966 this approach was virtually unheard of (certainly when applied to fine artists without any music biz experience), so instead he attempted to interest an established label in the album. But Reed's lyrics and the band's image were too daunting for both Atlantic and Elektra, and no deals were forthcoming. Then Tom Wilson, a young black producer at Columbia who'd worked with Dylan and Simon & Garfunkel, heard the record. Wilson was leaving Columbia to set up a rock division for the jazz label Verve (whose only other rock signing was The Mothers Of Invention) and offered the Velvets a deal, buying the tape outright (Warhol always claimed he never saw a penny in producer's royalties). But Wilson wanted some changes. He also felt there was "not enough Nico"; for him, she was the star attraction (see comments on 'Sunday Morning' below). Ironically, she and the Velvets would part company soon after, many months before the album's release.

But the release of the album was delayed and delayed, until the following Spring. This was due to (a) Verve's nervousness about the subject matter of material, (b) production problems with the cover's peelable banana sticker and (c)

The Mothers Of Invention having a pushy manager, who made sure *their* album came out first. In 1966, the year they were 'hot', the only Velvet Underground product made available would be 'Noise' and 'Loop' (two improvisational, feedback-based pieces given away free with - respectively - the *East Village Other* and *Aspen* magazine) and two singles taken from the forthcoming album ('All Tomorrow's Parties' and 'Sunday Morning').

When it *was* finally released, Verve promoted the album as a Warhol artefact. One ad in *Evergreen Review* read: "What happens when the Daddy of Pop Art goes Pop Music? The most underground album of all! It's Andy Warhol's new hip trip to the subterranean scene." But far from giving them credibility, at the time their association with Warhol meant that many critics refused to take them seriously, assuming the whole thing was just a camp put-on. As Sterling Morrison recalled, they found themselves regarded as "some phoney band that that phoney painter cooked up in New York. What did

we gain? We gained all his enemies – the people who thought he was a faker thought we were fakers."

What few reviews they got were bad, regarding the band's songs about drugs and sex as proof of true evil. Lou Reed: "Back then we were surprised at how vast the reaction against us was. I thought we were doing something very ambitious and I was very taken aback by it. I used to hear people say we were doing porn-rock." But the fact that Reed had used a first-person narrative caused many listeners to assume this was autobiography, rather than a literary device. Sterling Morrison later noted: "We played in a band, and had songs about things that we saw around us. It was not intended as a lifestyle for people to adopt, had no credos, no sets of rules. We never expressed it, but in a sense we, I think, demystified rock and roll."

Then came what Morrison has called "the crowning moment of doom". Eric Emerson, one of the Warhol crowd, sued Verve for using a photo without his permission on the album sleeve (he was part of a crowd scene). Sterling Morrison: "Emerson got busted with about 1,000 hits of acid, and was desperate for some money. Seeing how no one asked him about putting his picture on the cover, he asked Verve for a lot of money. Verve got scared and airbrushed it out." Verve responded by recalling some copies of the album, stickering others, and reprinting the cover – all of which caused a further delay in distribution. Eric Emerson died of a drug overdose shortly afterwards.

What with one thing and another, the record (comparatively speaking) sank without trace. But its time would eventually come. Brian Eno once said something to the effect that while the album's sales weren't huge, everyone who heard it subsequently went out and formed their own band. He may well be right. And it may well be an ongoing process.

The one area where Warhol did undeniably make an important contribution was the album's cover, which he designed. With its famous yellow silk-screened banana sticker which, when you peeled slowly, you saw revealed a pink banana underneath, the cover has become a memorable and elegant icon. (Warhol designed several other album covers over the years : for John Cale's 'The Academy In Peril', for The Rolling Stones' 'Sticky Fingers' and 'Love You Live', and for the posthumous John Lennon album 'Menlove Ave'. The cover for 'White Light/White Heat' was executed by Billy Name, from a "concept" by Warhol).

and nail to get poor Nico on."

Supposedly written by Reed and Cale in a friend's apartment at 6 a.m. one Sunday morning, after being up all night, it's a gentle, folksy ballad of paranoia and reassurance. According to Sterling Morrison it's "about how you feel when you've been up all Saturday night and you're crawling home while people are going to church. The sun is up and you're like Dracula, hiding your eyes." "It's pretty paranoid," admitted Reed.

SUNDAY MORNING

Added after the initial sessions at the request of Tom Wilson, who'd intended Nico to sing it, for release as a single. When the time came, Reed insisted on singing it himself. Paul Morrissey: "Tom Wilson couldn't deal with Lou, he just took what came. Then later, he got Nico back into the studio and gave her a verse or put her with Lou's voice or something, I can't quite remember. Tom Wilson had to force Nico to take this option, you can imagine. We were always fighting tooth

I'M WAITING FOR THE MAN

Driving urban blues that sounds as desperate as its subject matter (an account of scoring heroin in Harlem). Reed later observed that twenty-six dollars won't get you much of anything these days but that "everything about that song holds true, except the price". "PR shoes" refers to Puerto Rican Fence Climbers, an imaginative (if racist) nickname for the pointy-toed shoes known in Britain as winklepickers.

Nico (who didn't take heroin until sev -

eral years after she left the Velvets): "I wanted to sing Lou's song 'I'm Waiting For The Man', but he wouldn't let me. I guess he thought I didn't understand its meaning, and he was right. And we had the song 'Heroin', which I thought was a provocation. I really took little notice about these things, because they wouldn't let me sing properly. But I have to say that Lou and John took heroin, and the songs were songs of realism."

Lou Reed: "I did go down Lexington. I did all the stuff then."

FEMME FATALE

Lou Reed: "Andy's title." Though Reed has sometimes claimed that this is about Nico, most often he's admitted that he wrote it at the request of Andy Warhol, about Edie Sedgwick. A Massachusetts débutante from a rich but troubled socialite background, Sedgwick had spent her late teens in a mental institution (as had several of her brothers, two of whom committed suicide). In 1964, at the age of 21, she moved to New York and met Warhol in early '65 ; for the next year,

they were virtually inseparable. She dyed her hair to match his silver wig and became a kind of mirror image, escorting him to society parties. "She had more problems than anybody I'd ever met,'" Warhol later said. Perhaps that was part of the appeal of their relationship, which was certainly not sexual (Truman Capote thought that Andy wanted to *be* Edie).

She became the 'face' of young Manhattan; *Vogue* magazine dubbed her a 'youthquaker', and she seemed the archetypal poor little rich go-go girl. Bob Dylan was said to have loved her (according to some, both 'Just Like A Woman' and 'Leopard Skin Pillbox Hat' are about her), and he wasn't alone. But though undeniably beautiful, Edie was not so much *femme fatale* as *femme catastrophique*. Though she became a mainstay of Warhol's movies and danced on stage with the Velvets during their first couple of gigs, most of the time she was out of her head on a cocktail of drugs of every description, prescribed by the legendary Dr Roberts (immortalised by The Beatles). She later blamed Warhol for her condition: "Warhol really fucked up a great many people's - young people's - lives. My introduction to heavy drugs came through the Factory. I liked the introduction to drugs I received. I was a good target for the scene. I bloomed into a healthy young drug addict."

"Edie never grew up," Warhol responded (probably accurately) ... though such quotes as "a girl always looks more beautiful and fragile when she's about to have a nervous breakdown" don't show him in too sympathetic a light, either. When she left him in 1966, Warhol joked bleakly to playwright Robert Heide: "When do you think Edie will commit suicide? I hope she lets us know so we can film it." After Warhol, Edie attempted to carve a career as an actress (but didn't really have the talent) and model (but her reputation as an unreliable druggie preceded her), without success. She died in 1971 of a barbiturate overdose, at the age of 28.

Reed's ethereal ballad (sung by Nico) is a cautionary tale, almost a protest song.

VENUS IN FURS

A celebration of sado-masochism (and fetishist clothing), on which Cale's viola really comes into its own. Written by Reed after he'd read the novel by Leopold von Sacher-Masoch, the song basically recounts the story (Sterling Morrison called it "a musical synopsis") of Severin and his cruel mistress Wanda, who whips him while dressed in furs. The novel was supposedly at least semi-auto-biographical; Sacher-Masoch considered himself the 'slave' of Baroness Bogdanoff. In concert with the E.P.I., during this song Gerard Malanga would kneel and kiss Mary Woronov's black leather boots, while she lightly whipped his back.

Lou Reed: "I just thought it would be a great idea for a song. Now everybody thinks I invented masochism."

Sterling Morrison: "The band never set out to be devoted to sexual weirdness. It was a purely literary exercise... We do love songs of every description. 'Venus In Furs' is just a different kind of love song. Everybody was saying this is the vision of all-time evil, and I always said, 'Well, we're not going to lie.' It's pretty. 'Venus In Furs' is a beautiful song. It was the closest we ever came in my mind to being exactly what I thought we could be. Always on other songs I'm hearing what I'm hearing, but I'm also hearing what I wish I were hearing."

RUN RUN RUN

More urban blues - but done in an almost Dylanesque way - this time about the perils of New York's Union Square, infamous as a hangout for drug-dealers and junkies. Guitar feedback heightens the mood of manic paranoia. Written during the group's residency at the Café Bizarre in December 1965, when they realised that they were desperately short of original material.

Sterling Morrison: "Lou usually would have some lyrics written, and something would grow out of that with us jamming. He was a terrific improvisational lyricist. I remember we had the Christmas tree up, but no decorations on it. We were sitting around busy writing songs, because we had to, we needed them that night !"

ALL TOMORROW'S PARTIES

Cale's insistent piano drives this plaintive social lament, which might also be about Edie Sedgwick - or about Andy Warhol. Straight out psychedelic folk-rock, and "Andy's favourite song," according to Reed. Which figures - its Cinderella imagery would certainly appeal to a man nicknamed Drella. "A very apt description of certain people at the Factory at the time," is all Reed would say.

The CD release replaces the original vinyl version of this song with a 'previously unreleased' one. Both feature the same Velvets' backing track, but where the original featured Nico's vocals double-tracked, the CD has her singing 'solo' (as it were). It's not an improvement, but the situation would be rectified on the 'Peel Slowly And See' boxed set.

HEROIN

Lou Reed: "At the time I wrote 'Heroin', I felt like a very ... rather negative, strung-out, violent, aggressive person. I meant those songs to sort of exorcise the darkness, or the self-destructive element in me."

Maureen Tucker: "I consider that our greatest triumph. Lou's greatest triumph too, maybe, song writing-wise."

Written by Reed while he was still in college. He'd spend a sizeable chunk of his career having to account for it, as he commented in 1996: "I'd have to sit there with people saying, 'Don't you feel guilty for glamorising heroin, for all the people who've shot up drugs because of you?' I get that to this day, even though I didn't notice a drop-off in the sales of narcotics when I stopped taking things."

Lou Reed: "It was about what it's like to take heroin. It wasn't pro or con. It was just about taking heroin, from the point of view of someone taking it... I always used to say, 'If this was a book, you would not consider this shocking. *What* is shocking about it?' And I'm still not sure what was such a big deal. So there's a song called

'Heroin'. So *what?*"

Moe Tucker's persistent drumming keeps pace throughout with the increasing tempo of Reed's strumming; coupled with Cale's seesawing viola, they vividly conjure the desperation implicit in the lyric. The first time you hear it, it's awesome.

Lou Reed: "It's just two chords. And when you play it, at a certain point there is a tendency to lean in and play it faster. It's automatic. And when I first played it for John, he picked up on that. Also, if you check out the lyrics, there are more words as you go along. The feeling naturally is to speed up."

Tucker: "It's a pile of garbage on the record... The guys plugged straight into the board. They didn't have their amps up loud in the studio, so I couldn't hear anything. *Anything*... And when we got to the part where you speed up, you gotta speed up together or it's not really right. And it just became this mountain of drum noise in front of me. I couldn't hear shit ... So I stopped, and being a little wacky, they just kept going, and that's the one we took."

THERE SHE GOES AGAIN

A re-working of Marvin Gaye's 'Hitchhike', and a pretty straightforward Buddy Hollyish pop song. Except for its call for misogynist violence as a solution to relationship problems.

Morrison: "Metronomically, we were a pretty accurate band. If we were speeding up and slowing down, it was by design. If you listen to the solo break on 'There She Goes Again', it slows down – slower and slower and slower. And then when it comes back into the 'bye-bye-byes', it's double the original tempo. We always tinkered with that."

I'LL BE YOUR MIRROR

Folksy love song, written for/about Nico? According to Victor Bockris, Lou Reed had started writing it two years earlier, and it was about his girlfriend at Syracuse, Shelley Albin – though Nico came up with the title. The lyric could just as easily be about deep friendship as about romantic love. Reed later described it as "very compassionate, very loving, very nice."

Sterling Morrison: "Nico had two voices. One was a full-register, Germanic, *Götterdämmerung* voice that I never cared for, and the other was her wispy voice, which I liked. She kept singing 'I'll Be Your Mirror' in her strident voice. Dissatisfied, we kept making her do it over and over again until she broke down and burst into tears. At that point we said, 'Oh, try it just one more time and then fuck it – if it doesn't work this time we're not going to do the song.' Nico sat down and did it exactly right. As for the haunting quality in her voice, it's not because she's singing to Bob Dylan or Lou Reed. Nico was just really depressed."

THE BLACK ANGEL'S DEATH SONG

The song that got the group fired from their residency at Café Bizarre. Reed later commented that "the idea here was to string words together for the sheer fun of their sound, not any particular meaning. I loved the title." Over Cale's swooping viola, Reed rapidly intones lyrics rich in imagery; comparisons with Dylan would be inevitable (though Delmore Schwarz was probably his main influence).

Sterling Morrison: "A good friend of ours who saw many shows (and even played bass in one at the Dom), Helen Byrne, ran up to me after the release of the album and exclaimed, 'The Black Angel's Death Song – it's got chords!' Apparently she hadn't noticed in the live performances. 'Of course it's got chords,' I replied. 'It's a song, isn't it?"

EUROPEAN SON

Driving psychedelia, dedicated to Delmore Schwarz. Ironically, the poet hated rock music – which he called "catgut music" – especially the lyrics, which explains the sparsity of the words here. The vocal part sounds like a boogie version of one of Dylan's 'put down' songs; but most of this is devoted to feedback, guitar solo and general experimentation (which eventually just runs out of steam, or so it sounds). Just after the vocal part you can hear John Cale scrap-

ing a chair across the floor, at which point, according to Tucker: "He stops in front of Lou, who drops a glass, or a bottle, whatever it was... The engineer, my God, he's saying, 'What are you doing?' It was tremendous, because it is in time, and the music starts right up. I don't know how we timed it like that... ('European Son') was just different every time. There was no structure, we just did it."

Sterling Morrison: "'European Son' is very tame now. It happens to be melodic, and if anyone actually listens to it, 'European Son' turns out to be comprehensible in the light of all that has come since – not just our work, but everyone's. It's that just for the time it was done it's amazing. We figured that on our first album it was a novel idea just to have long tracks. People just weren't doing that – regardless of what the content of the track was – everyone's album-tracks had to be 2:30 or 2:45. Then here's 'European Son', which ran nearly eight minutes. All the songs on the first album are longish compared to the standards of the time."

WHITE LIGHT/WHITE HEAT

THE VELVET UNDERGROUND

825 119-2

WHITE LIGHT/WHITE HEAT

(VERVE V/V6-5046 ; RELEASED JANUARY 1968. CD : VERVE 825 119-2).

Personnel : John Cale (vocals, electric viola, organ, bass) ; Sterling Morrison (vocals, guitar, bass) ; Lou Reed (vocals, guitar, piano) ; Maureen Tucker (drums).

Sterling Morrison: "In the 'White Light/White Heat' era, our lives were chaos. That's what's reflected in the record."

Between the recording of the first album and its release, The Velvet Underground's world went through some major changes. Nico was (not too subtly) elbowed out, but with her gone, the group felt less musically compromised. "I was glad to see Nico go," said Tucker. "To me she was just a pain in the ass."

More painfully, they parted company with Andy Warhol. Lou Reed: "Andy came up to me and said we should have a talk. He said, 'You have to decide what you want to do, Lou. Do you want to start expanding into the outside world, or do you want to keep doing museums and art shows?' And I decided: 'Well, we're leaving you.' He was furious."

After Warhol's death, Reed reminisced affectionately: "Sometimes, when I'd got to the Factory early, there would be Andy hard at work on a silk-screen. I'd ask him why he was working so hard and he'd say, 'Somebody's got to bring home the bacon.' Then he'd look at me and say, 'How many songs have you written today?' I'd lie and say, 'Two' ... Andy was incredibly hard-working and generous. He was the first to arrive for work at The Factory and the last to leave. And then he would take us all to dinner. He gave everyone a chance. When he told me I should start making decisions about the future, and what could be a career, I decided to leave him. He did not try to stop me, legally or otherwise. He did, however, tell me that I was a rat. I think it was the worst word he could think of."

Until the writing sessions for 'Songs

For Drella', John Cale wasn't even aware that it was Reed who had instigated this parting of the ways. "I thought Andy quit," he said.

But they needed someone to assume his role (and hopefully improve upon it). Brian Epstein briefly seemed interested in them (though he was probably more keen on handling their song publishing than in managing them), but this came to nothing (and Epstein died shortly afterwards). Recognising that they needed a businessman (rather than a creative artist) to talk to the music business, in the summer of 1967 they appointed Steve Sesnick, a Boston club owner, to look after their affairs. Though they were all happy with this choice at the time, that was something that would change, and drastically. Suffice it to say that John Cale later called Sesnick "a snake"; and Lou Reed would subsequently place the blame for 'destroying' The Velvet Underground squarely on Steve Sesnick's shoulders.

Meanwhile, though their album wasn't selling brilliantly (and certainly wasn't getting any airplay), they managed to make a small living by touring almost constantly. Such would be the case for the rest of their brief career.

But they still experimented. Once, when Lou Reed was laid up with a bout of hepatitis, they tried a complete re-structuring. Angus MacLise was briefly re-recruited on drums, with Moe Tucker switching to rhythm and bass, freeing Cale for keyboards and viola. He also took all lead vocals. For obvious reasons, Reed wasn't too happy with this line-up (and MacLise departed as soon as Reed was well again), but Sterling Morrison felt it had real potential: "We were continually refining. I still think our best performances were never recorded." An improvisation piece conceived during this interlude called 'Searchin'' would eventually metamorphose into 'Sister Ray' (sometimes performed live with an improvised prelude titled 'Sweet Sister Ray', both parts being of indeterminate length).

John Cale was also keen to keep their creative edge sharp: "I had no intention of letting the music be anything other than troublesome to people. It was a revolutionary, radical situation. We really wanted to go out there and annoy people."

The material they came up with for their second album is certainly not as immediately user-friendly as their début. Creatively, John Cale admits that he and Reed were "at each others' throats" during this period (though amazingly they still managed to do some co-writing), something he blames largely on the stress of touring.

John Cale: "The album was very much thrown together... I think most of it happened on the road. That was about the time that the incoherence of our thinking about where the band should go started laying claim to a lot of our time."

The quarrels about musical direction would lead to Cale's departure within the year. They were protracted, and loud. Sterling Morrison: "Everyone in The Velvet Underground was strong willed, but Moe took a quiet role in our conflicts. She always said there was no reasoning with any of us, that we were all crazy, and there was no sense in arguing.

I think basically the band had three uncontrollable personalities, and if you throw drugs into the confusion, then you really have problems."

Part of the problem, according to Morrison, was that they never knew how Lou Reed was going to react: "Will he be boyishly charming, naïve – Lou can be very charming when he wants to be – or will he be vicious? And if he is, then you have to figure out what's stoking the fire. What drug is he on, or what mad diet? He had all sorts of strange dietary theories. He'd eat nothing, like live on wheat husks. He was always trying to move mentally and spiritually to some place where no one had ever gotten before."

Out of all this energetic antagonism came a record that M.C. Kostek accurately described as sounding like "sonic war". 'White Light/White Heat' stays in the urban reality Reed had been exploring to date, but now it sounded a lot more menacing. It's uneasy listening (if not a war, it's at least a duel), delivered at loud volume and high speed; it's heavy metal with brains (and a lot of problems).

As John Cale later admitted, "It was a very rabid record. The first one had some gentility, some beauty. The second one was consciously anti-beauty."

'White Light/White Heat' was recorded at Mayfair Sound Studios in New York during September 1967. Again produced by Tom Wilson, and engineered by Gary Kellgren. It's been claimed the band recorded the entire album in under three days. According to Moe Tucker it took "approximately seven sessions over a period of two weeks"; even so, as she admits, "It was a quickie." John Cale has implied that the time factor was a deliberate artistic choice, rather than a limitation imposed by poverty: "When it came to 'White Light/White Heat', it was like a road band improvising songs on stage... We decided to make that album as live as possible. We told Tom Wilson we were gonna do it as we do it on stage."

And they did – but the result was murky in the mix, with a *lot* of distortion and feedback. Sterling Morrison: "There was fantastic leakage because everyone was playing so loud and we had so much electronic junk with us

in the studio – all these fuzzers and compressors. Gary Kellgren the engineer, who is ultra-competent, told us repeatedly: 'You can't do it – all the needles are on red.' And we reacted as we always reacted: 'Look, we don't know what goes on in there and we don't want to hear about it. Just do the best you can.' And so the album is all fuzzy, there's all that white noise... We wanted to do something electronic and energetic. We had the energy and the electronics, but we didn't know that it couldn't be recorded... What we were trying to do was to really fry the tracks."

The album's black on black cover depicted a skull (a tattoo belonging to either Billy Name or Joe Dallesandro); design was by Billy Name from a 'concept' by Andy Warhol.

WHITE LIGHT/WHITE HEAT

Written by Lou Reed. A hymn to amphetamine; a gently pounding rock/folk thrash that would end up influencing everybody from The Rolling Stones to 'Ziggy'-era Bowie to The Ramones.

THE GIFT

The 'lyrics' to this were originally a short story written by Reed for creative writing class during his last year as an English major at Syracuse University, and it was possibly inspired by 'The Lottery', a Shirley Jackson short story. This macabre little tale of the unfortunate Waldo Jeffers and his love for Marsha reads like a cross between Roald Dahl and Stephen King; it was set to music at the suggestion of John Cale, who also narrates the piece, his Welsh accent heightening the sense of the bizarre. Cale read the whole thing through in one take. The music (credited to all four Velvets) grew out of an instrumental called 'Booker T' (see 'Peel Slowly And See'), so called because it was, according to Tucker, "inspired by Booker T & The MG's 'Green Onions'" – and it does actually sound a bit like an extended soul workout. The track was mixed so that Cale's voice comes out of one speaker, and the music comes out of the other. "So you could listen to one or the other or both," Reed later explained. Tom Wilson: "And if you're a mad fiend like we are, you'll listen to them all together. That's where we're at. We got stereo prefrontal lobes."

Lou Reed: "One of the things I've always regretted is that when Waldo gets stabbed in the head, I put a wrench into a cantaloupe on the track, and you can't really hear it. It's supposed to go 'squish'. It wasn't loud enough."

LADY GODIVA'S OPERATION

A baroque Gothic horror piece that prefigures some of John Cale's later solo work but was actually written by Lou Reed. Referring to the use of sound effects, John Cale described the piece as "a BBC Radiophonic Workshop idea". Some think this is about a sex-change operation, but the description here sounds even grislier – as with 'The Gift', this is not one for the squeamish. Reed subsequently blamed the twenty-four shock treatments he'd had when he was seventeen for causing him to write songs

like this one. He also said the song was about "fear of sleep. The perfect thing for the people we were running around with, staying up fifteen days at a time."

HERE SHE COMES NOW

Words by Reed, music by all four Velvets. Probably written with Nico in mind (she sang it in concert, but by the time they came to record it she was long gone), but sung here by Reed in folksy/blues mode. The only 'pretty' song on the record.

I HEARD HER CALL MY NAME

Written by Lou Reed. A rocker so fast-paced it's practically manic, with Reed eventually going truly berserk on the guitar. It seems to be about love beyond the grave - though whether that means necrophilia, or just sorrow for a dead love is something left to the listener's imagination.

Maureen Tucker: "Ruined in the mix –

the energy. You can't hear anything but Lou. He was the mixer in there, so he – having a little ego-trip at the time – turned himself so far up there's no rhythm, there's no nothing."

Sterling Morrison: "I quit the group for a couple of days because I thought they chose the wrong mix for 'I Heard Her Call My Name', one of our best songs that was completely ruined in the studio."

Lou Reed: "I was using these little hand-held Vox distortion effects. They actually plugged right into the guitar. They hit it and it went 'SHRIEK !' I was definitely in control of it."

SISTER RAY

Words by Reed, music by all four Velvets. Lou Reed: "If 'Sister Ray' is not an example of heavy metal, then nothing is." It's also totally uncompromising. Even to the most casual listener, the lyrics are *obviously* depicting hard drug use and homosexual activities. Musically, it's structured mayhem, with Cale's R&B organ vying with the two guitars for your attention while everybody meanders to and away from the tune; somehow, Tucker holds it all together.

Lou Reed: "I wrote the lyric – I think – while we were riding to and from a gig. I just wrote it out straight. It has such an attitude and feel to it, even if you don't understand a word of it. It sounds sleazy... It's just a parade of New York night denizens. But of course, it's hard to understand a word of it. Which is a shame, because it's really a compressed movie."

Reed would also suggest that 'Sister Ray' was built around a story he wrote about a scene of total debauchery and decay. "I like to think of Sister Ray as a transvestite smack dealer. The situation is a bunch of drag queens taking some sailors home with them and shooting up on smack and having this orgy when the police appear. And when it came to putting the music to it, it just had to be spontaneous. We turned up to ten, flat out, leakage all over the place. That's it. (The record company) asked us what we were going to do. We said we were going to start. They said "'Who's playing the bass?' We said, 'There is no bass'. They asked us when it ends. We didn't know. 'When it ends, is when it ends.'"

Admitting that lyrically this was "a graphic song," Reed recalls Warhol telling him, "'Oh, Lou, make sure that you make them do the sucking-on-my-ding-dong song'. So we did it. Seventeen minutes of violence... everyone was surprised." Reed later said that musically he was trying to create the rock 'n' roll equivalent of Ornette Coleman. Unable to agree on an arrangement, the band decided to record the song in one take – during which, according to Reed, the engineer actually left the studio ("He just said, 'Let me know when it's over'").

Maureen Tucker: "We blew the studio away, recording at one volume – live. We didn't think to work the mix because, see, we didn't know what we were doing." Tucker still complains that Tom Wilson hadn't turned on one of her drum mikes: "(He) was more interested in the blondes running through the studio." Lou Reed : "Maureen was perfect on 'Sister Ray'... All we wanted was someone who could play the telephone book."

THE VELVET UNDERGROUND

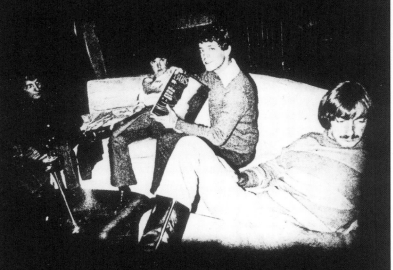

815 454-2

THE VELVET UNDERGROUND

(MGM SE 4617 ; RELEASED MARCH 1969. CD : VERVE 422-815454-2).

Personnel : Sterling Morrison (guitar) ; Lou Reed (vocals, guitar) ; Maureen Tucker (drums) ; Doug Yule (vocals, bass, organ, piano).

The Velvets spent most of 1968 on the road, promoting 'White Light/White Heat'; but once again, they got virtually no reviews or radio airplay, and once again the record was not distributed terribly well. But live, they were in their element.

Sterling Morrison: "Our touring was successful and our playing was excellent. Perhaps the possibility of real success suddenly became so tangible that we pursued it into megalomania and ruin. Our struggles to succeed on our own terms, once directed outwards at audiences, record execs, radio stations and whatnot, perhaps turned inward toward the group, with unfortunate consequences."

The problem was that Cale and Morrison wanted the band to go further in the same direction 'White Light/White Heat' was heading, while Reed wanted to do something radically different.

John Cale: "There were a lot of soft songs and I didn't want that many soft songs. I was into trying to develop these really grand orchestral bass parts. I was trying to get something big and grand and Lou was fighting against that. He wanted pretty songs."

Lou Reed: "I really didn't think we should make another 'White Light/White Heat'. I thought it would be a terrible mistake, and I really believed that. I thought we had to demonstrate the other side of us. Otherwise, we would become this one-dimensional thing, and that had to be avoided at all costs."

Sterling Morrison: "(Cale) was going in a more experimental direction, while Lou wanted something within a more 'pop' context... John and I were very happy with 'Sister Ray'-type music... Lou placed heavy emphasis on lyrics. Cale and I were more interested in blasting the house down."

Recording sessions took place in February and May that year, but nothing led anywhere (the results can be heard on 'VU' and 'Another View'), presumably because of these tensions between Reed and Cale.

John Cale: "They were creative conflicts. I think egos were getting bruised." They were unable to reconcile their differences, Cale finding Reed impossible to deal with ("Maybe it was the drugs he was doing at the time. They certainly didn't help").

But while the Velvets were busy touring and scrapping over musical direction, their former manager was lying in hospital. On June 2, 1968, Andy Warhol became the victim of a near-successful assassination attempt. Though deeply shocked when he heard of the incident, for some reason Lou Reed did not go to visit Warhol in hospital – something over which he would suffer guilt pangs for years to come.

In August 1968 the Reed/Cale crisis finally came to a head. Reed convened a meeting with Morrison and Tucker, informing them that he wanted Cale out of the group, for good. This didn't go down too well. Sterling Morrison: "I was enraged! To me it was unthinkable. I really laid into Lou." But Reed told them he'd rather dissolve the Velvets completely than continue with Cale, and the others eventually acquiesced. Sterling Morrison: "Now, I could say that it was more important to keep the band together than to worry about Cale, but that wasn't really what decided me. I just wanted to keep on doing it. So finally I weighed my self-interest against Cale's interests and sold John out."

John Cale went quietly, and with as much dignity as he could muster ("Lou and I eventually found the group too small for both of us, and so I left"), playing his last gig with the group that September. He would subsequently state his opinion that the 'VU' had "never really fulfilled our potential". The reasons, he claimed, were that "drugs, and the fact that no one gave a damn about us, meant we gave up on it too soon."

Sterling Morrison stayed angry at Lou Reed for years over this (and the fact that he continued to hang out socially with Cale only increased Reed's paranoia). Maureen Tucker reluctantly accepted the situation ("I was so sad when John went. I always wished he was over there, flailing away on his viola"), but stated later: "I would have liked to have had the opportunity to do even one more album with John. We were all much more attuned to each other after two years than on the first album."

As a replacement, the band brought in Doug Yule, a 21-year-old bass player from Boston who'd been in a group called the Glass Menagerie. Later on, his organ-playing would go some way to becoming a worthy substitute for Cale's viola drone-effects.

Though Sterling Morrison was seemingly the one to discover Yule, Lou Reed was thrilled with the choice, finding the new bass player a refreshing change: "I was working with Doug's innocence... I'm sure he never understood a word of what he was singing. He doesn't know what it's about. I mean, I thought it was so cute... I adore people who are like that."

But for the others, there were reservations. Sterling Morrison: "It was never the same for me after John left. He was not easy to replace. Dougie was a good bass player, and I liked him, but we moved more towards unanimity of opinion. I don't think that's a good thing. I always thought that what made us good were the tensions and oppositions. Bands that fight together make better music." Tucker feared that Reed's flattery would go to Yule's head and cause yet more problems, thus adding the gift of prophecy to her other talents.

When the time came for them to record again, the group ran into a technical hitch *en route* to the studio in California. Sterling Morrison: "All our effects boxes were locked in a munitions box that was stolen at the airport when we were leaving for the West Coast to record. We saw that all our tricks had vanished, and instead of trying to replace them, we just thought what we could do without them." What Morrison and Reed did was to kit themselves out with twin Fender 12-string guitars. The new album would be as quiet as its predecessor was loud, and be comprised of new material, most of which had never been performed live.

In fact, much of it hadn't even been written. The group stayed at the Château Marmont in LA, where they wrote and rehearsed during the afternoons; they would then record the songs at night. Lou Reed: "It might be the most purely 'studio' album we ever made. We never played 'Jesus' before. 'The Murder Mystery' was performed seldom even after that, because of the recitation. 'Afterhours' had never been recorded before, because Maureen is too shy to sing it. In fact, when she recorded it, everybody had to leave the studio."

Sterling Morrison: "We did the third album deliberately as anti-production. It sounds like it was done in a closet – it's flat, and that's the way we wanted it. The songs are all very quiet and it's kind of insane. I like the album."

Doug Yule: "The grey album was a lot of fun. The sessions were constructive and happy and creative. Everybody was working together."

All songs were by Lou Reed, and many of them were more personal-sounding, and dealt with love and sex. According to Victor Bockris, many had their genesis in Lou's on-again-off-again relationship with his old girlfriend Shelley Albin. Reed has stated that the songs can be seen as one large story cycle.

The imaginatively titled 'The Velvet Underground' (sometimes known as 'the grey album', on account of the colour of the cover) was recorded in November and December 1968 at TTG Studios, Hollywood. "Arranged and conducted" by The Velvet Underground, assisted by engineer Val Valentin.

Confusingly, there are two different versions of this album: a mix done by Lou Reed, which was used for the original vinyl release, and a mix done by Valentin (used for the CD re-release). Valentin's mix was done first; after which Reed returned to the studio with the tapes and did his version, christened the 'closet mix' by Sterling Morrison: "I thought it sounded like it was recorded in a closet. Why did he do it? I don't know, specifically. To judge from the result, to bring the voices up and put the instruments down. I guess he felt the real essence of the tracks was the lyrics."

Morrison's analysis succinctly underlines the difference between the two mixes. Valentin's version is more orthodox (and reveals instrumentation inaudible on the closet mix, like a bass on 'Afterhours'), but I have to say I prefer Reed's version – it's much clearer and cleaner. Valentin's remains available as the standard CD release, but at Reed's insistence it would be the 'closet mix' that was chosen for inclusion in the 'Peel Slowly And See' boxed set.

CANDY SAYS

Gently sad ballad of self-despair. Doug Yule takes lead vocal, as Reed had strained his voice singing live. Reed described it at the time as "probably the best song I've written." "Candy" was Candy Darling, a drag queen and Factory 'superstar' from Long Island (real name James Slattery), who later died from cancer caused by silicon breast implants or hormone injections (accounts differ). Reed would later refer to her again, using her as one of the characters in his solo hit 'Walk On The Wild Side'. But dissatisfaction with self-image is something not confined solely to drag queens, as Lou Reed observed: "All of us have said at some point, 'I wish I was different. I wish I had curly hair, or straight hair'. Whatever. I don't know a person alive who doesn't feel that way. That's what the song is really about – and not only in looks, but in what you require."

WHAT GOES ON

Rocking pop song about being messed about (and up) by love. The first line echoes The Beatles' song of the same title; 'Lady Be Good' is the title of a song by George & Ira Gershwin.

Doug Yule: "Lou cranked his guitar up all the way and played a solo. It was good, and we said, 'wanna try another?' We got a few more tracks, and we put down three solos. He came back in and listened, and the engineer said, 'well, the next one you do, we'll have to kill another one, because we don't have any more open tracks.' This is in the days when you didn't have unlimited tracks. So I said, 'Why don't you play one more, and we'll play them all at once.' And it worked. It sounds like bagpipes."

SOME KINDA LOVE

Bluesy (and darkly comic) exhortation to sexual experiment.

The lyric echoes T.S. Eliot's *The Hollow Men*: "Between the idea/And the reality/Between the motion/And the act/Falls the Shadow." Reed would later use 'Between Thought And Expression' as the title for both his 1992 CD retrospective, and his collection of selected lyrics.

Lou Reed: "I think one of the greatest parts (Sterling) ever did was what he played on 'Some Kinda Love'. It's like a

perfect clock. It just goes on and on and on. You can move around it all you want, and it's anchored in there. Everything revolved around that part, and even though it's repeated, it seems to change as you listen to it."

The CD (Valentin mix) features a completely different take to the 'closet mix'.

PALE BLUE EYES

Perhaps Lou Reed's most haunting ballad, gently and delicately arranged, 'Pale Blue Eyes' is a song of yearning loss; the relationship is doomed because it is adulterous (according to Victor Bockris, Shelley Albin, now married to someone else, had briefly but disastrously resumed her affair with Reed). Written, according to Reed "for someone I missed very much. Her eyes were hazel. It's been recorded by a lot of people, but my favourite version is by Maureen Tucker." Tucker's version (on which Reed plays guitar) is on her 1989 solo album 'Life In Exile After Abdication'. The lyric echoes both 'I'll Be Your Mirror' and the title of a novel, Richard Farina's *Been Down So Long It Looks Like Up To Me*.

Sterling Morrison: "That's a song about Lou's old girlfriend in Syracuse. I said, 'Lou, if I wrote a song like that, I wouldn't make you play it.' My position on the album was one of acquiescence."

JESUS

A gently beautiful plea for redemption which surprised even Lou Reed: "When I wrote 'Jesus', I said, 'My God, a hymn!'" It hovers somewhere between folk, country-blues and gospel.

BEGINNING TO SEE THE LIGHT

A bouncy, optimistic rocker that sounds almost a variation on 'I'm Waiting For The Man', but is a lot more joyous.

I'M SET FREE

Another driving rocker, but the exultant title is misleading – this is about heartbreak and pain, as the mournfully bluesy guitar solo attests. The relationship is over; the best that can be hoped for is another one, but even that will just be another "illusion".

THAT'S THE STORY OF MY LIFE

Bouncealong honky tonk vaudeville, which contrasts sharply with the bleakness of the previous song. The "Billy" referred to – and quoted from – in the lyrics is Factory photographer Billy Name (real name Billy Linich). As a reliable guide to morality, one should bear in mind what Reed later pointed out: "He also told me I was a lesbian, so you have to take things with a grain of salt."

THE MURDER MYSTERY

Another experimental track, with two sets of 'lyrics' – recorded and mixed so that one set would emanate from each speaker, with the music in the middle. Sung by the entire band. "I was having fun with words and wondering if you could cause two opposing emotions to occur at the same time," Reed would later explain. The stream-of-consciousness lyrics were subsequently published as a poem – or rather, two parallel poems – in the Winter 1972 issue of *The Paris Review* (#53). What it's about, one wonders if even Reed knows. He later told Lester Bangs: "When I did that song, I dismissed decadence." Sterling Morrison has described his guitar riff here as "sort-of like the fright music in a B-movie serial". The music here comes perilously close to being jazz-rock.

For Reed, it was a failed experiment: "Good try, but it didn't work. It couldn't be recorded that well. The idea was simple – have two lyrics running at the same time, so you get hit with one monologue in one ear and the other monologue in the other ear, like two guitar parts. Just as two guitar parts are supposed to interweave, so are these two poems. But it didn't work because you couldn't hear either one well enough to hear what was being said."

AFTER HOURS

A song of loneliness, and in praise of the solace found in alcohol ; for those whose local bar has become the only bright and friendly place in the world. Sung by (and composed for) Moe Tucker, who makes her vocal début here. The Valentin mix sounds like more honky tonk vaudeville; Reed's mix sounds like folk/blues. "I loved after-hours bars," Reed explains in *Between Thought And Expression*, going on to tell an anecdote about Nico which you should buy his book to read.

Lou Reed: "It's a terribly sad song, and I didn't sing it because I figured people wouldn't believe me if I sang it. But I knew Maureen for instance had a very innocent voice."

Maureen Tucker: "I like the song. I like

the words. I was just very nervous recording it. I tried it about eight times. Finally, I made everyone leave. It was just me, Lou and the engineer, and I finally did it okay. But I told them, 'I'm not doing this live unless some-one requests it'. Because I was scared stiff. Then some creep requested it in Texas. So that was my singing début on stage."

Lou Reed: "You still don't hear that kind of purity in vocals. It has nothing to do with singing. It has everything to do with being. It's completely honest. Guileless. And always was. I couldn't sing that song. Maureen could sing it, and believe it, and feel much more. Because it's about loneliness. 'Someday I know someone will look into my eyes' – it can be so sappy and trite. But with Maureen doing it, especially being just a little off-key, it has its own strength and beauty and truth to it."

LOADED

(COTILLION SD 9034 ; RELEASED SEPTEMBER 1970. CD : WARNER 9-27613-2).

Personnel : Sterling Morrison (guitar) ; Lou Reed (guitar, piano, vocals) ; Billy Yule (drums) ;
Doug Yule (organ, piano, bass, drums, lead guitar, guitar, vocals).

On various dates between May and October 1969, The Velvet Underground recorded what would come to be regarded as their 'lost' MGM/Verve album. Maureen Tucker: "That was the best session, with Gary Kellgren of the Record Plant, who died, drowned in his pool. Young guy, extremely helpful, a real nice guy, engineer, producer. We recorded in New York, six or eight days, tremendous." But whether the tracks were ever actually intended for an album is a little unclear. The group were trying to get free from MGM (who hadn't given them much support, financial or otherwise), and they did contractually owe the label one more album. It seems unlikely they were recording just for the fun of it, but on the other hand their first three albums had been badly-promoted and ineffectively distributed, and as Maureen Tucker points out, "We weren't that interested in giving them another one to just let die."

The material they recorded then would subsequently surface on bootlegs and - much later - on the 'VU' and 'Another View' albums. In the end – and quite probably *before* they had finished what they set out to do in the studio – MGM dropped them from their roster. At that time MGM President Mike Curb issued a statement, which read in part: "Groups that are associated with hard drugs... are very undependable. They're difficult to work with, and they're hard on your sales and marketing people." With this attitude as their new company policy, it's easy to see not only why MGM dropped the Velvets, but also why they chose not to release the already-recorded material they had in their vaults.

Amazingly, it took the group several months to find a new record deal, before they eventually signed a two-album contract with Atlantic. So, The Velvet Underground returned to New York, to record at Atlantic Studios. Recording took about ten weeks (between April - July 1970). Production would eventually be credited to Geoffrey Haslam, Shel Kagan and The Velvet Underground; with Adrian Barber as engineer.

Mysteriously, in the main they chose not to re-record the songs they'd already recorded for MGM; the finished 'Loaded' included only 'Rock & Roll' from the 'lost' album, plus nine *new* songs. This may have been because they still believed that MGM might release the earlier recordings, or because they were legally prevented from re-recording that material. The latter seems unlikely – for one thing, they *did* also re-record 'Ocean' (though it wouldn't surface until 1995's 'Peel Slowly And See'), and Reed was certainly free to re-record much of the material for his first solo album in 1972. It seems more likely that the group were just disenchanted with the 'lost' songs, or found them tainted by the move from MGM, and

wanted a fresh start.

But from the start, they were beset with problems. Firstly, Sterling Morrison had taken a step back from band politics, and seems to have been largely unaware of the arguments that would soon boil over. He'd taken advantage of the group's prolonged stay in New York to take some academic courses, and had his head in a book most of that summer. Consequently, as he later noted: "It wasn't really apparent to me that we were falling apart."

Secondly, the band were still touring fairly constantly, and during the course of recording they played a gruelling ten-week-long summer residency at Max's Kansas City, playing live five nights a week. As a result of this, Lou Reed strained his voice once again, and the group were forced to let Doug Yule sing lead on several tracks. Sterling Morrison: "Lou simply does not have that durable a voice. He was so ragged on some of the cuts that we either had to stop the production, or let Doug take over. But no one preferred to have Doug sing."

The result, according to Reed, was that "the sense that the songs were handled and interpreted in got changed. Like, 'New Age' was supposed to be funny – a girl thinking she was like a movie queen and the guy down the block was Robert Mitchum. And 'Sweet Nuthin' was even more different – it was intended as a sly song making fun of some people that it describes, and not at all the sort of very serious statement it ultimately became."

Thirdly – and perhaps worst of all – they'd lost Moe Tucker. Though she gets a credit on the sleeve of 'Loaded', she was actually absent throughout recording. In March she'd taken a leave of absence because of her first pregnancy, and had been (temporarily) replaced on drums by Doug Yule's younger brother Billy for the duration of recording. The album sleeve also credits "percussion assistance" to session drummer Tommy Castanaro and engineer Adrian Barber. To this day, Tucker is annoyed that she didn't get to play on the record.

Had Tucker been there, she might have been a calming influence. One was certainly needed because of their fourth major problem: manager Steve Sesnick. Sesnick had been pushing Reed to become more of a showman; at the same time he'd also been encouraging Doug Yule to take a more prominent role in the group. Whether he intended it or not, the result was that Sesnick drove a wedge between the two. As a result – with Tucker elsewhere and Morrison seemingly uninterested – Reed felt not only betrayed by the people he had relied on as allies, but totally isolated as well. He later squarely blamed Sesnick for what was to follow: "It became less fun when we had a manager. I think he destroyed the group. He took two or three years, but he destroyed it and made it so it wasn't fun any more, so I quit."

Moe Tucker later placed more blame on Doug Yule than on Sesnick, recalling that when Doug had joined the band in '68 "we all thought he was great – a great guitar player, bass player, singer. But within a year he'd become an asshole... in my eyes, and I believe, in Lou's and Sterling's. It was a lot of subtle things. If a new song came along, he'd be on bass, usually, with Sterling on guitar. Without being invited, Doug would pick up a guitar and start creating a part for himself. Many times Sterling would have to tell him, 'Hey, you're the bass player'...

"We all wondered why Lou would put up with this, for years. Why didn't he just say, 'I want him out of the band'? We were all so damned sick of him, we would have jumped on it. But he just let it build up... personally, I think the real reason he finally left was Doug. I didn't see this as a big plot on the part of Steve Sesnick. But, yes, the moment Lou was gone, Steve clearly picked out Doug as the next 'star'. He took over the vocals and started writing some songs. There seemed to be a lot of ego-petting. Maybe he felt Doug would simply be a lot easier to manipulate."

The atmosphere in the studio must have been pretty terrible. Sesnick even briefly brought in John Cale, in an attempt to reignite former glories (which probably only increased Reed's paranoia), a fact which didn't even surface until 1995.

In August, Lou Reed could stand it no longer, and quit the group. His later comments seem to indicate that Sesnick had smelled impending success with the new record, and was greedily pushing the group places Reed wasn't too sure he wanted to go. Lou Reed: "I gave them an album loaded with hits, and it was loaded with hits to the point where the rest of the people showed their colours. So I left them to their album full of hits that I made."

The following month 'Loaded' was released – though Lou Reed had had no say in the running sequence, and was far from pleased with the production and mixing, citing in particular the "severe" editing of 'Sweet Jane' and 'New Age'. He later commented: "If I could have stood it, I would have stayed there and showed them what to do." To his ears, the finished product was concrete proof of a "conspiracy" against him. But Sterling Morrison later defended the mixing, and the engineers involved: "'Loaded' is incomparably the best mix of any of our albums. Lou had no control over the mix, and if Geoffrey Haslam and Adrian Barber were involved in such a 'conspiracy', why did the work come out sounding better than anything else?"

Ironically, despite all the obstacles stacked against it, 'Loaded' is a bright and breezy collection of outright pop songs, and easily the most commercial record The Velvet Underground ever made. And it paid off – the record even got radio airplay, and reviews were uniformly positive. Lenny Kaye wrote in *Rolling Stone*: "Easily one of the best albums to show up this or any other year."

All of this Lou Reed must have found bitterly ironic. Worse, though, the album sleeve credited "song composition" to Reed, Morrison and Yule, and "lyrics" to Reed and Yule, crediting Reed last each time. Lou Reed sued, claiming the songs were entirely his work; he (eventually) won back the rights to the songs – and legally freed himself from his management contract with Sesnick – but was denied control of the 'Velvet Underground' name, enabling Yule to continue using it long after the event.

Doug Yule later stated that he'd had "a significant influence on Lou. Lou and I had significant influence together on the group. I, of course, did no more than Lou – he was doing the writing, I was arranger, musical director. I was handling my half, he was handling his. Many said Lou was The Velvet Underground, and in a sense that it was his brainchild, he was – he was the main force behind it, but it was a band, and like any band its totality is made up of all its members, not just one person with side musicians."

And as Sterling Morrison later pointed out, "Lou really did want to have a whole lot of credit for the songs, so on nearly all of the albums we gave it to him. It kept him happy. He got the rights to all the songs on 'Loaded', so now he's credited for being the absolute and singular genius of the Underground, which is not true. There are a lot of songs I should have co-authorship on, and the same holds true for John Cale. The publishing company was called Three Prongs, because there were three of us involved.

I'm the last person to deny Lou's immense contribution and he's the best songwriter of the three of us. But he wanted all the credit, he wanted it more than we did, and he got it, to keep the peace."

Lou Reed spent the next year or so working as a typist for his father's accountancy firm. When he re-surfaced as a solo artist in early 1972, it was on his own terms. "It was a process of elimination from the start," he said. "First no more Andy, then no more Nico, then no more John, then no more Velvet Underground."

WHO LOVES THE SUN

Deceptively cheerful (and poppy) ode to nature, sung by Yule. Despite the sting in the lyric (as P.G. Wodehouse once observed, the sun always shines when your heart is broken), the fact that the Velvets were singing about something as good-time as sunshine at all was pretty astonishing. As with several of the songs here, this has a vaguely countryish feel, reminiscent of the music The Grateful Dead were making that same year.

SWEET JANE

Based around a rhythm riff that's practically a Reed trademark, this verges on the anthemic. This time, the song's protagonist 'outsider' (a rock musician) is looking 'inwards', examining the lives of his more orthodox friends (a banker and a clerk), perhaps with envy, perhaps not.

'Sweet Jane' would develop into a punk rock standard with numerous spikey- haired bands essaying its simple chord structure at the close of their shows. Notable non-punk covers include Mott The Hoople's rousing effort in the early Seventies and The Cowboy Junkies smooth, laid back interpretation in the Eighties.

ROCK & ROLL

Like most of his generation, Lou Reed discovered rock 'n' roll via the radio, and this nostalgic celebration of the medium is practically autobiography. First recorded for the 'lost' album, a version that would eventually surface on 'Another

View'. This one has a more epic, joyous feel to it, plus some extremely tasteful guitar work. Then again, it *doesn't* have Moe Tucker.

Lou Reed: "'Rock & Roll' is about me. If I hadn't heard rock & roll on the radio, I would have had no idea there was life on this planet. You know what I'm saying? Which would have been devastating - to think that everything everywhere was like it was where I came from. That would have been profoundly discouraging. Movies didn't do it for me. TV didn't do it for me. It was the radio that did it."

Sterling Morrison: "We had the radio, and DJs like Alan Freed and Jocko Henderson. We could hear all that music coming from New York City. And what New York represented to me as a kid from Long Island – it was way beyond Oz."

COOL IT DOWN

Exhortation to relaxation, though whether it's about drugs or sex is anybody's guess... though 'Miss Lindy Lee' would seem to be a hooker (he waits for her "on the corner", and she loves him "by the hour"). Honky tonk piano by Yule; the vocal sounds like Reed double-tracked.

NEW AGE

Practically the screenplay for a movie, this tale of a movie star past her prime and her younger lover is evocative in mood of Billy Wilder's *Sunset Boulevard*. If that movie *was* an influence on Reed, then he produced a *far* more appealing (and catchy) adaptation than Mr Lloyd Webber did twenty years later. The tone here is appropriately mock-epic, approaching gospel territory towards the end. Vocal by Yule.

Lou Reed: "No slur on Doug, but he didn't understand the lyrics for a second."

HEAD HELD HIGH

Enjoyably nonsensical R&B about self-respect (not to mention posture awareness). They almost sound like the Stones here.

LONESOME COWBOY BILL

Supposedly about William Burroughs, author of *The Naked Lunch* and elder statesman of beat culture – but it's hard to see any connection to him in this country-rock number (complete with Reed yodelling) about a rodeo rider.

I FOUND A REASON

Graceful torch song, which could easily have fitted on the third album and sounds so personal (despite the self-mocking spoken middle section) that Reed must have winced at Yule's vocal interpretation (however good it was, it could never have been good enough).

TRAIN AROUND THE BEND

According to Moe Tucker, this is about the Long Island railroad. A song about going home to New York, after too long on the road. The guitar at the start of this sounds disconcertingly like John Cale's viola.

OH! SWEET NUTHIN'

Bittersweet countryish blues about poverty (something the Velvets knew a lot about). Vocal by Yule.

THE VELVET UNDERGROUND LIVE AT MAX'S KANSAS CITY
Featuring: Lou Reed, Doug Yule, Billy Yule, Sterling Morrison

max's
kansas city

LIVE AT MAX'S KANSAS CITY

(COTILLION SD 9500 ; RELEASED MAY 1972. CD : ATLANTIC 7567-90370-2).

'I'm Waiting For The Man'/'Sweet Jane'/'Lonesome Cowboy Bill'/'Beginning To See
The Light'/'I'll Be Your Mirror'/'Pale Blue Eyes'/'Sunday Morning'/'New Age'/
'Femme Fatale'/'Afterhours'.

Ultra Violet: "Max's Kansas City is where the Pop scene, Pop life, and Pop Art fuse. It is a two-storey restaurant and bar at Park Avenue South and Sixteenth Street, the big hangout of the Sixties. Mickey Ruskin, the owner, has operated previous establishments – Deux Magots on East Seventh Street, the Paradox, the Ninth Circle, the Annex – that attracted poets, poetry readings, painters, sculptors. At Max's the heavyweights of the art world hang around the long bar, and in the back room, kids, groupies, dropouts, beautiful little girls of fourteen who've already had abortions, get noisy or stoned."

Andy Warhol: "Everybody went to Max's, and everything got homogenised there."

As previously stated, during the Summer of 1970 the Velvets played a ten-week residency at the club, towards the end of which Lou Reed quit the band. "I hated those last bookings at Max's," he later stated. "I couldn't do the songs I wanted to do, and I was under a lot of pressure to do things I didn't want to do - and it finally reached a crescendo. I never in my life thought I would not do what I believed in, and there I was, not doing what I believed in, that's all, and it made me sick."

Although released by Atlantic, the 'Live At Max's' album is effectively a bootleg. The band knew nothing about it, and it was recorded on a very basic cassette player (a Sony TC120) belonging to the group's friend (and Warhol 'superstar') Brigid Polk (a.k.a. Berlin). Supposedly this is a recording of the band's set made on August 23, 1970, Reed's last night with the Velvets, though there's nothing to confirm that it wasn't recorded some other night before Reed's departure.

Polk's tape recorder had just been lying on a table, and the tape is pretty appalling in terms of technical quality. It's in mono, and the audience is frequently louder than the group. But with Reed gone, Danny Fields persuaded Polk of the tape's value as the group's last recording; they sold the tape to Atlantic for $10,000 outright (which they split between them). Atlantic released it despite the band's objections, claiming it as the second album they'd contracted for. It was released at a budget price, probably because Atlantic were conscious of the poor sound quality.

But despite the sound, 'Live At Max's' has several things going for it. On the downside, though Billy Yule is competent enough, he's certainly no replacement for Moe Tucker. But though the group sound fairly weary and ragged, what's amazing is how poppy and commercial they are, especially on the 'Loaded' material – they truly sound like they're on the verge of great things. Even Reed seems to be

enjoying himself; one can't help but wonder how successful they might have been if he'd stuck around a while longer.

Lou Reed: "The last night I was there, when Brigid made her tape, that was the only night I really enjoyed myself. I did all the songs I wanted – a lot of them were ballads."

And – even if you hate the rest of the record – at least you get to hear Lou Reed singing 'Afterhours' in a joyously cynical way (Tucker: "He sings better than I do".)

Moe Tucker was in the audience that night, taking time off from tending to her new baby to visit her old band. "I didn't hate it," she later said, "but it wasn't the Velvets. To me, there were only two Velvets there, Lou and Sterling. And it didn't work. It was a nice, tight little band. But it wasn't the Velvets."

After the show, Tucker learned of Lou's intention to quit the group: "Lou took me outside and told me he was leaving. I was heartbroken. But I knew something had gone terribly wrong, that he had to leave in order to survive the thing."

When Reed introduced Sterling Morrison to his long-estranged parents that evening, Morrison was baffled, and knew *something* very strange was occurring - but he would officially hear the news from Steve Sesnick: "He said, 'Lou's gone home and quit the band.' We finished the week at Max's without him." And that was that.

Though the group objected to the album's release (as they would – in varying degrees – with all the posthumous Velvets' releases between 'Loaded' and the 'Peel Slowly And See' boxed set), Reed would later acknowledge its worth: "The Max's live set, now that's another album I really love. If you want to know what Max's was really like – and now you can't – it's there, for real, because Brigid was just sitting there with her little Sony recorder. It's in mono, you can't hear us, but you can hear just enough. We're out of tune, per usual... but it's Sunday night, and all the regulars are there, and Jim Carroll's trying to get Tuinols, and they're talking about the war... We were the house band. There it is." Max's Kansas City closed its doors forever in December 1974.

Note: Brigid Polk recorded the whole show, but four tracks were left off the album release ('Who Loves The Sun', 'Cool It Down' and 'Candy Says'; the fourth song, 'Some Kinda Love', would eventually surface on 'Peel Slowly And See').

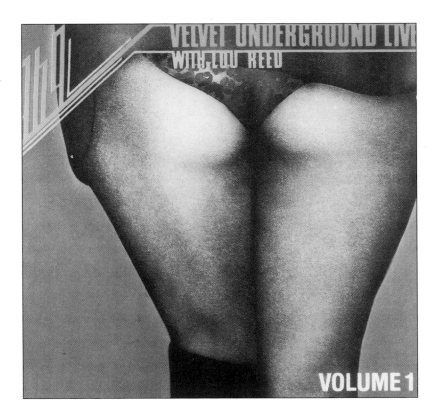

1969 : VELVET UNDERGROUND LIVE

(MERCURY SRM 2-7504 DOUBLE LP ; RELEASED APRIL 1974.
CD'S: MERCURY 834 823-2 AND 834 824-2).

VOLUME ONE: 'Waiting For My Man'/'Lisa Says'/'What Goes On'/'Sweet Jane'/
'We're Gonna Have A Real Good Time Together'/'Femme Fatale'/'New Age'/
'Rock And Roll'/'Beginning To See The Light'/'Heroin'.
VOLUME TWO: 'Ocean'/'Pale Blue Eyes'/'Heroin'/'Some Kinda Love'/'Over You'/
'Sweet Bonnie Brown'/'It's Just Too Much'/'White Light White Heat'/
'I Can't Stand It'/'I'll Be Your Mirror'.

As previously stated, The Velvet Underground were touring almost constantly during 1969. Five years later, this live double-album appeared. Reportedly it's drawn from over eight hours of tapes, but zero recording details were given on the sleeve. Some tracks are thought to have been taken from a gig at the Matrix in San Francisco, but the bulk of this album is supposedly drawn from an October, 1969 gig at the End Of Cole Avenue club in Dallas, Texas.

Lou Reed: "I think that night was the first night we'd ever played it. Some rich kid in Texas had a sort of club. If he liked a group, he'd bring them into the club and invite friends over. It was insane."

Sterling Morrison: "I don't like it, because it was recorded in small locations... Generally, our sound was bigger. On this record everything is subdued, there are no really loud songs." At least one other show was taped during this period, at the Vulcan Gas Company in Austin, Texas, but these tapes have been missing for years.

The tapes that would comprise '1969: Velvet Underground Live' had come into the possession of their old manager Steve Sesnick... but before he could release them commercially, he needed the permission of the band. Amazingly,

1969 THE VELVET UNDERGROUND LIVE: THE VELVET UNDERGROUND

Lou Reed agreed (the fact that his name appears in large print on the cover may have had something to do with it). And so, in early 1974, Sterling Morrison was surprised to discover his past resurfacing: "I started getting these calls from Steve Sesnick, and I thought, what is this bullshit? Then *Lou* even called. Apparently his lawyer had told him to turn on the charm. They wanted me to sign for the release of the '1969: Velvet Underground Live' album.

"I did *not* want it released... You know, there is a certain clean feeling that comes from not dealing with the people you'd have to, to collect royalties on anything like that. And I'd listened to the tapes and I thought – oh, man ! I can't see this selling ten copies. Musically, I much preferred 'Live At Max's' – it has much more energy. I said I was not going to go along with it.

"I was told if I continued with this attitude, dragging my feet, then the album wouldn't come out at all. I said I had no need to bolster a sagging career with something like this... but, fine, I hope you

put it out tomorrow so I can start suing you. Then Steve Sesnick finally convinced me. I signed the release for a pittance because he told me he needed the money. I'm sure he was in cahoots with Lou in some strange way. Meanwhile, Mercury had pressed ahead with the production. That's why I wasn't listed anywhere on the record, because I wasn't... co-operating."

According to Tucker, she and Morrison were originally offered the princely sum of $200 each to sign a release form so that the album could come out; they eventually agreed to $1,500 apiece.

Despite Morrison's assertion that "other performances on that tour are ten times better," the record is actually pretty stunning (despite having one of the tackiest covers of all time). For one thing, the sound quality is almost infinitely superior to the 'Max's Kansas City' album. And the band seem in good shape and humour – Reed chats away merrily with the audience, asking them what kind of gig they want. On 'Max's', he's barely

PAGE 50

able to complete a sentence.

More importantly, they're playing well. And for most listeners, this was the first chance to hear the Velvets really stretching out, and playing greatly extended versions of their album tracks (most of which were pretty long to start with). Doug Yule's extended organ forays (reminiscent of The Band's Garth Hudson) give songs like 'What Goes On' an added dimension, with the twin guitars constantly jockeying for position with him. The results are bluesy and energetic, and often surprising.

'Lisa Says' segues into another, more vaudevillian song (possibly titled 'Why Am I So Shy') before turning back into 'Lisa Says' again. There's a radically different version of 'Sweet Jane' – a lot gentler, and with completely different words. According to Reed, these are "the original lyrics, even recorded the day I wrote it". 'New Age' also has very different lyrics, name dropping "Frank and Nancy" (Sinatra, presumably) and generally sounding a lot more cynical and world-weary.

Several of the songs here were new to most listeners (at least, in the Velvets' versions – Reed had already re-recorded three of them as a solo artist: 'Lisa Says', 'Ocean' and 'I Can't Stand It', the last being added as a bonus track on the CD. Reed would re-record 'We're Gonna Have A Real Good Time Together' a few years later). Studio versions of those four would surface in time, but two songs remain available only in this recording (though both are unremarkable): 'Over You' is a gentle love song; 'Sweet Bonnie Brown/It's Too Much' is fast-paced R&B, but goes nowhere interesting.

Critically, the album went down extremely well. For reasons unknown, it took another five years for the record to be released in the UK. When it finally appeared, in 1979, British critical response was just as enthusiastic. Post-punk, the Velvets still looked good.

Annoyingly, when the time eventually came for a CD release, the double-album was released as two separate CD's. Two extra tracks ('Heroin' and 'I Can't Stand It') were added for the CD release.

the velvet underground

VU

823 721-2

VU

(VERVE 823 721-2 ; RELEASED FEBRUARY 1985).

A collection of previously unreleased recordings discovered in the Verve vaults during the process of re-issuing the first three Velvets albums on CD. Most of these were unmixed master tapes (only 'Ocean' had been properly mixed at the time); utilising state-of-the art technology, these tapes were cleaned up and mixed in June 1984. Most come from sessions for the 'lost' fourth Verve album, recorded at the Record Plant in New York between May and October 1969, and engineered by Gary Kellgren. The remaining two tracks come from a session with John Cale in New York in February 1968.

All songs presumably by Lou Reed (no credits are given) unless otherwise indicated; produced and arranged by The Velvet Underground. Remixed by Michael Barbiero at MediaSound in New York.

Critical reaction to this album was near-ecstatic – not simply because rock historians had been given a chance to indulge their nostalgia, but because the record was actually bloody good. As Allan Jones noted in *Melody Maker*: "Twenty years on, listening to The Velvet Underground is still like dancing with lightning... They remain, arguably, the most influential group in the history of rock."

I CAN'T STAND IT

Recorded 20/5/69. Irresistibly rocking Dylanesque lament of lost love; infinitely preferable to the version Reed would later record for his first (eponymous) solo album in 1972.

STEPHANIE SAYS

Recorded 13/2/68 at A&R Studios, New York. John Cale's haunting viola announces his presence at the start of this gently haunting lament of regret. The song would receive its first official outing (in drastically rewritten form) on Reed's

1973 solo album 'Berlin', though by that time the protagonist had changed her name, and the song was now titled 'Caroline Says II'.

SHE'S MY BEST FRIEND

Recorded 14/5/69. Unashamedly dumb beat group pop, and wonderful with it. As the vocal fades, Reed can be heard screeching gibberish in the background. Maureen Tucker: "I hated the ending, which I still do. I thought it was just tacky. Childish, you know, his vocal part." Re-recorded by Reed for his first solo album in 1972.

LISA SAYS

Recorded 1/10/69. Moody complaint of dissatisfaction in the quest for love and/or sex. Once again, Reed would rework this for his first solo album in 1972.

OCEAN

Recorded 19/6/69. The ocean as an analogy for madness, the protagonist

here eventually being engulfed by the waves (and/or his own nutso thought patterns). The gentleness of mood here just makes it all the more ominous. Another version of this was recorded during the 'Loaded' sessions (see 'Peel Slowly And See'). Lou Reed would also re-record the song yet again, this time for (you guessed it) his first solo album in 1972.

FOGGY NOTION

Recorded 6/5/69. 'Peel Slowly And See' credits this to Morrison, Tucker, Doug Yule and Hy Weiss. More dumb beatpop, this time positively dripping with lustful anticipation. Sterling Morrison: "I got to play all those leads, so I really like that. That was recorded totally live in the studio, voice and everything, which is why I was able to play underneath the vocal, sometimes even the same notes. I'd do that, then get bored and wander off someplace on the guitar."

TEMPTATION INSIDE YOUR HEART

Recorded 14/2/68 at A&R Studios in New York, once again with John Cale in the line-up. Spoof Motown, and irresistibly catchy despite Reed's unforgettable physics theory: "electricity comes from other planets". According to Morrison, the idle chatter and asides from the participants was unintentional, but accidentally ended up on the finished track. If so, Reed's vocal is presumably only a guide track for finished vocals that were never recorded.

Sterling Morrison: "We recorded the song and it was straightforward. Then me, Lou and John went into this tiny vocal booth, ostensibly to lay down the background vocal doo-doo-doo's. We're waiting for our big moment while the track is running, so there are these layers of comments. We thought, 'They'll just close the pot, and open it up at the right time'. So we're talking, general nonsense – Lou commenting, 'That's not a bad solo', stuff like that." In fact, the trio then returned to the booth to double-track more vocals,

and the same thing happened again... One of the comments, 'Shut the door', was Lou and me walking in there late. The track was already running. Finally, we hit the last notes and there's all this general laughing. My parting thing is, 'Was that awful?' I was referring not to the track, but to the harmonies. I never had any faith in our vocal harmonies."

ONE OF THESE DAYS

Recorded 23/9/69. A countryish blues, about being treated badly in love and drunkenly planning an exit. David Fricke reckons Reed's imitating a Hank Williams yodel-effect here, and he's absolutely right.

ANDY'S CHEST

Recorded 13/5/69. On June 3, 1968, Andy Warhol was the victim of an assassination attempt by Valerie Solanas, a would-be 'superstar' whose film script Warhol had rejected. She was also the founder of an extremist feminist group called SCUM (the

Society for Cutting Up Men), and was dangerously psychotic – Warhol later recalled that Solanas "would talk constantly about the complete elimination of the male sex". At four o'clock on the afternoon in question she followed Warhol into the new Factory offices at 33 Union Square West, waited until he had finished a phone conversation, and then pulled out an automatic pistol and fired three .32 calibre bullets into his chest and abdomen at point-blank range. Warhol was rushed to Columbus-Mother Cabrini Hospital, but pronounced clinically dead at 4.51 p.m. His chest was cut open, his heart massaged back to life, and five doctors spent the next five hours operating on his lungs, liver, gallbladder, spleen, intestines and pulmonary artery. Miraculously, Warhol survived – though his chest was criss-crossed with scars and he would suffer problems with digestion and sleeping for years to come, and had to wear a corset (to keep his stomach muscles in place) for the rest of his life.

Earlier that year Warhol had made his most famous (and most misquoted) remark: "In the future everybody will be world famous for fifteen minutes."

Ironically, his own shooting garnered not much more than fifteen minutes of press attention, since Robert Kennedy was assassinated the next day, pushing him out of the headlines. Though Warhol was forgiving towards his attacker ("I don't think Valerie Solanas was responsible for what she did. It was just one of those things"), most observers agree that he was visibly never the same after the shooting. Nor was he left unguarded or unprotected any more; security video cameras were installed at the Factory, where the 'open house' policy came to an end.

As to Valerie Solanas: she surrendered to police several hours after the shooting, and was remanded to Bellevue Hospital for psychiatric evaluation. Declared incompetent to stand trial, she pleaded guilty to "reckless assault with intent to harm", and was sentenced to three years in prison. She was released in September 1971, but spent much of the Seventies in mental hospitals. She died of bronchial pneumonia on April 25, 1988, fourteen months after Andy Warhol.

Lou Reed: "'Andy's Chest' is about

Andy Warhol being shot by Valerie Solanas, even though the lyrics don't sound anything like that." In fact, the song is a poetic reverie (its title possibly inspired by Richard Avedon's famous photo of Warhol displaying his scars) that makes no direct mention of the shooting or Warhol's wounds – it's just a deeply affectionate get-well-note from a one-time disciple.

The Velvet's version is minimalist folk/beat; when the song got its first offi-cial release (on Reed's second solo album, 1972's 'Transformer'), it acquired a much more lavish approach (courtesy of David Bowie's arrangement).

I'M STICKING WITH YOU

Recorded 13/5/69. Vocals by Moe Tucker (aided by the others) on a childlike (and gently melodic) affirmation of friend-ship/love which could have been unbearably fey; instead, it's utterly charming.

VELVET UNDERGROUND

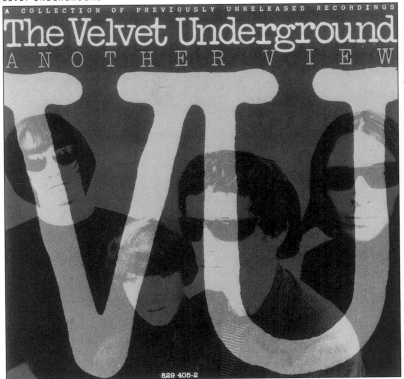

PAGE 60

ANOTHER VIEW

(VERVE 829 405-2 ; RELEASED JULY 1986).

Following the critical and commercial success of 'VU', the following year saw the release of a second batch of unreleased material from the Verve vaults. But this time – though many of the songs were still well up to par – one could also hear the sound of the barrel being scraped.

Utterly minimal sleeve notes are provided, the only clues as to the personnel involved being the recording dates. All songs were credited to The Velvet Underground. 'I'm Gonna Move Right In', 'Ferryboat Bill' and 'Rock And Roll' were all mixed at the time of recording; all other tracks were mixed during March 1986 by J.C. Convertino at Sigma Sound. As with 'VU', Bill Levenson was executive producer.

Maureen Tucker : "I liked 'VU' better than 'Another View'. Sterling likes 'Another View' better, which surprised me. His only complaint was that it had too many instrumentals. Then I read something where Lou said that he didn't like that idea too much either, but he could see where a fan would want to hear them even without vocals. It's true, and that's who the record is aimed at, people who have been fans already. But it's too clean. I just think the whole thing is too clean... I was not happy at all with the mix of 'Another View'. Not at all. I think they did a terrible job. Now, Sterling suggested they didn't have the original four-tracks, that maybe they just had the master or something, and they couldn't do anything about the mix, but I don't know."

According to Tucker, it may be that at least one other song was recorded for the 'lost' album: 'Lonesome Cowboys', written for Andy Warhol's movie of the same name and seemingly a different song to 'Lonesome Cowboy Bill'. Since the Warhol movie opened in May 1969, the song may have been recorded earlier; then again, Reed may have been as behind schedule as he was for Warhol's 'Chelsea Girls' (see 'Peel Slowly And See').

The success of both 'VU' and 'Another View' inevitably led to media speculation that The Velvet Underground might be persuaded to re-form. "It'll never happen," Lou Reed stated flatly.

WE'RE GONNA HAVE A REAL GOOD TIME TOGETHER

Recorded 30/9/69. Dance number that sounds positively frenetic compared to the limply mannered version Reed would record for his 'Street Hassle' album in 1977.

I'M GONNA MOVE RIGHT IN

Recorded 27/9/69. Fairly unremarkable instrumental, with much bluesy meandering.

HEY MR. RAIN (Version I)

Recorded 29/5/68 at T.T.G. Studios, Hollywood. John Cale's viola dominates this ethereal folk/blues ballad.

RIDE INTO THE SUN

Recorded 5/9/69. Exquisite guitar instrumental that starts off like surf music and ends up sounding like The Beatles (just listen to the piano and the drum fill).

CONEY ISLAND STEEPLECHASE

Recorded 6/5/69. Reed in vaudeville mood again; apart from being a fairly corny love song, it deliberately invokes nostalgia for a more innocent age. The 'Coney Island Steeplechase' was a mechanical horse ride; but Coney Island's heyday as an amusement park was before Reed was even born.

GUESS I'M FALLING IN LOVE
(Instrumental version)

Like it says, an instrumental version of a song they often played live (a 1967 live version surfaced on 'Peel Slowly And See'). Here it sounds like a fairly thrashy surf guitar instrumental. Recorded 5/12/67, and thus an out-take from 'White Light/White Heat'. If you want to hear the words, you'll find another vocal version on the 'Live MCMXCIII' album.

HEY MR. RAIN (Version II)
Recorded 29/5/68 at T.T.G. Studios, Hollywood. Slightly more upbeat version to the first one, but not quite as success-ful or atmospheric (it spends a fair amount of time just being shambolic).

FERRYBOAT BILL
Recorded 19/6/69. Throwaway self-indulgence, built around an incredibly lame joke.

ROCK AND ROLL
Recorded 19/6/69. The "original version"; more delicate (and less epic) than the version they'd record for 'Loaded', with great drum fills. I like it a lot.

THE VELVET UNDERGROUND - THE WILDERNESS YEARS

Lou Reed's departure was not quite the end of the Velvets as a functioning (if dysfunctional) band. And Reed would re-surface as a solo artist within the year, though Sterling Morrison declined an invitation to hitch up with him in a new band ("Maybe I should have done it," he admitted years later); instead, Morrison stayed on with Yule for another year, during which time Moe Tucker returned to the drum stool.

After Sterling Morrison finally left the group in 1971, he returned to full-time academia, teaching English Literature while studying for his doctorate in Medieval Literature at the University of Texas in Austin. After gaining his PhD in 1986, he commenced a new career as a tugboat pilot in the Houston Ship Channel. Improbable, but true.

With Morrison gone, Doug Yule attempted to keep the Velvets going by adding Boston musicians Willie Alexander and Walter Powers (both of whom had played in Glass Menagerie with him) and continuing to tour (with Moe Tucker, who subsequently regretted tagging along). Danny Fields nicknamed them "the Velveteen Underground". Yule also recorded one album using the Velvets' name, 1972's 'Squeeze', but by this time

Tucker, Alexander and Powers had all walked out. The record doesn't merit close examination, so I'm not going to give it any. In fact, it truly is The Velvet Underground in name only, since the only musician on it apart from Yule is session drummer Ian Paice (of Deep Purple). Both Yule brothers subsequently quit the music business. Doug Yule recorded two solo albums in the late '70s with a group called American Flyer, and – amazingly – also played on Lou Reed's 'Sally Can't Dance' album in 1974. He now has his own cabinet-making business, and fatherhood has replaced music as his main concern – though on occasion he still jams with friends, and with his brother Billy (about whom nothing else is known).

Maureen Tucker resurfaced with a

solo album, 'Playin' Possum' in 1982, followed by a couple of EP's. In 1989 she quit her job as a computer operator in a shipping warehouse in Arizona, and moved to Georgia; she also released another album, the splendidly-titled 'Life In Exile After Abdication' (on which Lou Reed guested), followed by another in 1991, 'I Spent A Week There The Other Night'. She even managed to coax Sterling Morrison back into music, and the two would tour together on several occasions. She is the mother of five children, and also undoubtedly the sanest person in this whole story.

Angus MacLise died in Kathmandu in 1979.

Nico's first solo album, 1968's 'Chelsea Girl' contained not only two songs recorded with the Velvets (both tracks since included on the 'Peel Slowly And See' boxed set, and discussed more fully there), but also several other songs written by Cale and Reed, plus two ballads by the 16-year-old Jackson Browne (reputedly one of her lovers) and the first outing of the song Bob Dylan

wrote for her, 'I'll Keep It With Mine'. Reunited with John Cale as producer for two underrated albums, 'The Marble Index' and 'Desertshore', Nico established her own unique style as a chanteuse of doom laden Gothic romances, accompanying herself on an Indian harmonium. But by 1974's 'The End' (also produced by Cale) she'd long-since begun her spectacular descent into alcoholism and junkiedom, and the rest of her career verged on self-parody. Aged 49, she died while on holiday in Ibiza on July 18, 1988, and was cremated in Berlin; none of The Velvet Underground nor anyone from the Factory attended her funeral.

John Cale's post-Velvets career is properly deserving of a book in its own right. As a producer, his credits include Jonathan Richman's Modern Lovers, Patti Smith, The Stooges, Squeeze, Ian Hunter and many more. He's collaborated with Brian Eno and Terry Riley, and played as a guest musician with (among others) Nick Drake, Mike Heron and William Burroughs. And he's produced a massive body of solo work - nineteen albums' worth - that's intelligent, thoughtful (and occasionally downright catchy). Yet commercial success has eluded him, and he remains determinedly maverick, as critic Mary Harron once observed: "John Cale, who was as brilliant as Lou Reed, has been more consistent (than Lou), but throughout his solo career he has not simply avoided success, but tried to throttle it with both hands." For those not already aware of his work, a 2-CD anthology 'Seducing Down The Door' (Rhino R2 71685) covers the years 1970-90, and provides a good place to start.

Lou Reed's solo career also merits a much longer account than we have room for here. He's collaborated with (among others) David Bowie, U2, The Tom Tom Club and Nils Lofgren. His second solo album yielded a massive hit in 'Walk On The Wild Side'; his subsequent career has been a roller-coaster of high and low points. By the time of punk, he seemed almost an anachronism to some, but his later work has been challenging, revealing and mature – to paraphrase the man him-

self, he's grown up in public. In 1992 he released a 3-CD retrospective boxed set, 'Between Thought And Expression' (also the title of a collection of his selected lyrics, published the same year), that distilled the best material from his first eighteen solo albums. His nineteenth, 1989's critically lauded 'New York' showed a drive and consistency many thought he'd lost (not to mention some damn fine tunes). The roll continued with his 1990 collaboration with Cale, 'Songs For Drella', and with 1992's 'Magic And Loss', which dealt with subjects generally ignored in rock: death and mourning. He has publicly allied himself with a number of social causes, most notably the anti-apartheid movement, Greenpeace, and Amnesty International (on whose behalf he toured the world).

Though various members of The Velvet Underground had collaborated on sundry solo projects, never had anything approaching the full band played together after 1970. The closest – and most dramatic – it ever came was in 1972, when Cale, Nico and Reed played a short set together at the Bataclan Theater in Paris. At that time, Reed suggested that they re-form the group, and the others turned him down. As time passed, positions and feelings changed; but Reed was no longer interested.

As the decades passed, the Velvets' critical reputation grew, as did the recognition of their influence and the size of their audience (which now spanned several generations). The posthumous live albums and out-take collections only fuelled the interest. And in 1986 they even got paid: a lawyer acting on behalf of Cale, Tucker and Morrison had managed to renegotiate their old record company contracts, as a result of which they started to finally receive royalty cheques. They'd waited a long time for them.

But no matter how large their following, no one ever really expected The Velvet Underground to reunite as a group. There were just too many disagreements, too much history and too much bad blood.

And then Andy died.

LOU REED/JOHN CALE

SONGS FOR DRELLA

LOU REED/JOHN CALE : SONGS FOR DRELLA - A Fiction

(SIRE/WARNER BROTHERS 7599-26140-2 ; RELEASED MAY 1990).

Andy Warhol had been ill for a long time. His gallbladder was badly infected, but he had steadfastly procrastinated about having the operation he knew was necessary (following his post-assassination experiences, he'd developed an – understandable – terror of hospitals). But the pain eventually became so bad that he could put it off no longer. After a three-hour operation on February 21, 1987, Warhol's gallbladder was removed and found to be gangrenous. Afterwards, he seemed to be recovering well, but he died – alone – early the following morning, seemingly of heart failure. There were rumours of AIDS (unlikely – sexually, Warhol was reportedly more voyeur than participant), and accusations of hospital incompetence or neglect (the subject of a malpractice lawsuit). Some thought Warhol must have awoken in the night and – not knowing where he was – simply died of fright.

Lou Reed had not spoken with Warhol in years, and their relationship had never really recovered from the managerial split. But he was still deeply saddened by Warhol's passing: "Andy had a great effect on my formative years. His way of looking at things I miss. I owe him that. His whole aesthetic. I still wonder, if I look at something new and interesting, oh, I wonder how Andy'd think about that." And – with almost poetic symmetry – Warhol's death brought him together with John Cale once again. They met at Warhol's memorial service.

Later that year, Cale began working on a musical tribute to Warhol – an instrumental piece, which Reed would later call "a mass, of sorts". In May 1988 Cale contacted Reed, and asked him to listen to the work-in-progress. The two started discussing Warhol and his impact on their own lives, and, as Reed would later put it, "the opportunity arose to do the bigger thing. We were both keen because, after talking at length about Andy, there seemed to be a great need for us to put the record straight. The things I was disturbed about with 'Drella' was these evil books presenting Andy Warhol as just a piece of fluff. I wanted to show the Andy I knew." And so Cale's mass began to metamorphose into a project that would become the 'Songs For Drella' song-cycle, later described by Reed as "a brief musical look at the life of Andy Warhol" and also "entirely fictitious." He'd also refer to it as "biorock". And though 'Drella' isn't a Velvets album as such, it's still pivotal to their story.

Lou Reed: "John and I just rented out a small rehearsal studio for three weeks, and locked ourselves in." Both men had had long musical careers since they'd parted company twenty years earlier; both had survived battles with drink and drugs and were now happily clean and sober. As Cale admitted, "We're bringing a lot of baggage to the project", but this time – though creative arguments would inevitably rear up – they were mature enough to work round them. While they were working on the project, there came the news of another death in the 'family';

now Nico was gone as well.

John Cale: "It began as just the two of us throwing ideas around, but gradually it turned into song writing… I was really excited by the amount of power just two people could do without needing drums, because what we have there is such a strong core idea that the simpler the better … Although I think (Lou) did most of the work, he has allowed me to keep a position of dignity in the process." The entire work is co-credited. But the lyrics were all Reed's work, and he found it "an excruciating son-of-a-bitch to write. I did it on my word processor – what a tool! – and had to do rewrite after rewrite. And all the time I was finding out more about what I really felt about Andy and trying to put that into the right words."

The results paid off. Few people have ever been given such a touching and intelligent eulogy, though it's far from being all sunshine and light – in the course of it, Reed spares neither Warhol nor himself. Yet throughout, Warhol's own talent and humour shines through, as does Reed's evident (though ambivalent) affection for his subject. Why 'Drella'? Appropriately, Warhol's nickname was a blend of Cinderella and Dracula. Lou Reed: "Andy did some incredibly generous things for me. But he had made it clear he was not some mutant artist-father responsible for all of us. This often resulted in cruelty, but I agreed with his position."

Reed later stated that 'Songs For Drella' had been "written for the stage", and that's where it was honed. An incomplete version of the work was first performed in January 1989 at St. Ann's Church in Brooklyn, Reed's home turf. Reed then spent several months on the road, promoting his 'New York' solo album; when the duo were reunited later in the year he'd refined the lyrics, and also added the pivotal 'A Dream'.

In December 1989 they premièred the completed 'Drella' with a four-night run at the Brooklyn Academy of Music; on the last night Maureen Tucker joined her ex-cohorts on stage for an encore rendition of 'Pale Blue Eyes'. The next day, they performed the song cycle once again, this time in front of the video cam-

eras, for a later commercial release. On film the duo are professional, confident, assured, with a rapport that verges on the telepathic, and where each nod speaks volumes.

Of Warhol, the inspiration of it all, Reed said simply and eloquently: "We miss him very much."

Still, Reed insisted there would be no further collaborations. John Cale (despite saying shortly after the album's completion, "working with Lou is never dull, but I wouldn't want to go through it again") was more optimistic: "Now that we've accomplished that and shown that we can do it, we can move ahead to something more challenging. Collaboratively, I think Lou and I could come up with something very imaginative that would be more in the form of a dramatic situation. We're really efficient, and I think we could do anything. I don't think there's a limit."

SMALLTOWN

The overview of Warhol's life and work kicks off with his childhood... but though Warhol sometimes claimed to come from a small town (McKeesport, Pennsylvania), in reality he'd grown up in Pittsburgh. Which isn't exactly small, though the Big City would remain New York (echoing Reed's own upbringing). As with most of the songs here, Reed sings in the first person *as* Warhol.

Lou Reed: "Where I grew up I think of as an all-time hell-hole. When I wrote 'Small Town'... that's what that was about. That was a good song – kind of my answer to Mellencamp's song of the same name."

OPEN HOUSE

In which Warhol's enduring love of (and need for) company is explored, as well as his early career in New York.

STYLE IT TAKES

John Cale takes over Andy's role for an exploration of some of Warhol's most famous work, and of how he could sweet talk and flatter whatever (money, space, a performance) was required out of whoever was being asked.

WORK

Abandoning the Warhol persona, Reed recounts some of his own memories of Warhol – including those to do with the managerial split – centred around the artist's workaholic nature.

Andy Warhol: "Why do people think artists are special? It's just another job."

TROUBLE WITH CLASSICISTS

Cale returns for a comparative analysis of artistic methods and their failings.

STARLIGHT

Back to Reed for an exploration of Warhol's films, his approach and attitudes to the medium, and to 'stardom'.

Whoever walked through the Factory's doors – be they complete nobodies or Dali, Duchamp and Dylan – they were expected to endure a screen test (Dylan objected).

FACES AND NAMES

Cale-as-Warhol again. Though Warhol was seemingly incessantly drawn to fame and beauty, many claim he treated *everybody* alike. The fact that he had a terrible memory for names might explain his view that life would be a lot simpler if we were all interchangeable.

Andy Warhol: "If everybody's not a beauty, then nobody is."

IMAGES

A viola-drone riff dominates, as Reed-as-Warhol defends his most famous stylistic trademark: multiple images of the same thing, each subtly different from the others.

SLIP AWAY (A WARNING)

In which Reed-as-Warhol is warned that the Factory is getting out of hand, but refuses to listen.

IT WASN'T ME

In which Reed-as-Warhol denies responsibility for the high mortality rate (suicides and drug-related deaths) around him.

Andy Warhol: "Now and then someone would accuse me of being evil – of letting people destroy themselves while I watched, just so I could film them and tape record them. But I don't think of myself as evil – just realistic. I learned when I was little that whenever I got aggressive and tried to tell someone what to do, nothing happened – I just couldn't carry it off."

Andy Warhol: "When people are ready to, they change. They never do it before then, and sometimes they die before they get round to it. You can't make them change if they don't want to, just like when they do want to, you can't stop them."

I BELIEVE

Reed abandons the Warhol persona and personally enters the fray, describing Valerie Solanas' assassination attempt, Warhol's injuries and recuperation, and his own feelings of a need for retribution – that Solanas got off way too lightly – and guilt that he never visited Warhol in hospital. (See also the entry for 'Andy's Chest' on 'VU'). He also states outright that it was "the hospital" that eventually killed Warhol.

NOBODY BUT YOU

"There is nothing like getting shot to kill a party," as Nat Finkelstein bitchily observed. After the shooting, most observers agree, Warhol was a completely different person: Andy II, who went to parties and had dinner but produced (for him) very little worthwhile work. Reed's lyric explores Warhol's own reactions to his new life... and the mood is one of utter, crippling, isolation. Reed-as-Warhol vocal.

A DREAM

"This is not an excerpt from Andy's diaries," Reed wrote in *Between Thought And Expression*. Reed had been appalled by the shallow inanity and bitchiness of *Warhol's Diaries*, (something he'd emphasise on 'Hello, It's Me') and wove verbatim quotes from the book (including Warhol's remarks about himself and Cale) into a monologue that reveals much (both good and bad) about what Warhol was actually like as a person. "I wrote this trying to capture the love of the Andy I knew both inside and out," Reed later wrote. Though Reed has performed this live on solo tours, here it's Cale who takes the vocal, his Welsh lilt heightening the dreamlike atmosphere. Added in its later stages, this became the album's centrepiece and undisputed gem.

Lou Reed: "It was John's idea. He had said, 'Why don't we do a short story like "The Gift"?' But then he went away to Europe saying, 'Hey, Lou, go write a short story.' But I thought, no, not a short story – let's make it a dream. That way we can have Andy do anything we want. Let me

tell you, man, it was really hard to do. But once I got into Andy's tone of voice, I was able to write for a long time that way. I got to the point where I was able to, you know, just zip-zip-zip away – just because I really liked that tone so much. It's certainly not my tone of voice at all. I really don't talk that way. I had to make myself get into that way of talking."

FOREVER CHANGED

Cale-as-Warhol, on the different changes his life passed through – including, presumably, the final one. There is, of course, an album by Love entitled 'Forever Changes' – but the use of the past tense here underlines the sense of finality.

HELLO, IT'S ME

The most personal (and moving) song here, as Lou Reed bids a final farewell to his one-time mentor.

LIVE MCMXCIII

(SIRE/WARNER BROS 9362-45464-2 ; RELEASED OCTOBER 1993).

DISC ONE: 'We're Gonna Have A Real Good Time Together'/'Venus In Furs'/'Guess I'm Falling In Love'/'Afterhours'/'All Tomorrow's Parties'/'Some Kinda Love'/'I'll Be Your Mirror'/'Beginning To See The Light'/'The Gift'/'I Heard Her Call My Name'/'Femme Fatale'.
DISC TWO: 'Hey Mr. Rain'/'Sweet Jane'/'Velvet Nursery Rhyme'/'White Light/White Heat'/'I'm Sticking With You'/'Black Angel's Death Song'/'Rock 'N' Roll'/'I Can't Stand It'/'I'm Waiting For The Man'/'Heroin'/'Pale Blue Eyes'/'Coyote'.

Although 'Drella' had certainly augured well for future collaborations, few (including the band) could have guessed that it might lead to a full-scale Velvet Underground reunion. Reed and Morrison hadn't even talked to each other in years (royalties and song writing credits being the principal bones of contention).

Then, in June 1990, Reed, Cale, Tucker and Morrison all agreed to attend the opening of a Warhol/VU retrospective exhibition organised by the Cartier Foundation, just outside Paris. Still, even when he arrived there Reed was insistent that "you'll never get the four of us together on one stage again... ever. The Velvet Underground is a story," and Sterling Morrison held out until the very last moment. But on the opening day Reed mellowed, inviting the others to have lunch with him. That afternoon (June 15) Cale and Reed performed five-songs from 'Drella' in front of 300 invited guests (journalist, mainly)... and then Tucker and Morrison joined them on stage for a 15-minute version of 'Heroin'. No rehearsal, no sound check, just straight in at the deep end. Naturally, the crowd went nuts.

Afterwards, an exhilarated Cale stated, "Three hours ago this was not possible. Now, I'm overcome with emotion." "That was extraordinary," said Reed. "To have those drums behind me, that viola on one side, and that guitar on the other again – you have no idea how powerful that felt." Maureen Tucker was similarly exultant, while Morrison commented simply: "Not bad. Was I in tune?"

What were they like? Reviewing the event, Nick Kent wrote: "It was ample enough demonstration of a musical chemistry that still smoulders after 22 dank, mostly bitter years apart."

Now the ice had been broken. They spent several days together, and met again several times over the course of the next few years. But nothing of note happened until December 1992, when the band got together to discuss several pending projects (including Sterling Morrison's history of the band – provisionally titled *The Velvet Underground Diet* – and a retrospective boxed set). At the meeting Lou Reed joked that they ought to play Madison Square Garden for a million dollars. Maureen Tucker: "It was just a joke, but was the first time any of us had said anything like that in front of the

other three. After a lot of thought, we all decided, 'Yeah, a Velvets reunion is a really cool idea.'" Within two months the four were rehearsing for a European tour.

Sterling Morrison later told David Fricke: "It was pride that kept us apart. But it was also pride that made us do well. Nobody cares more about our legacy than we do."

That the motive for the reunion may have been largely financial scarcely mattered to their expectant audience. And after all, some of them truly needed the money – Moe Tucker didn't even own a car, let alone a house. She confessed to Max Bell: "The money aspect is like winning the lottery to me." Sterling Morrison had to take six weeks off work as a tugboat pilot in order to tour, but he didn't quit the day job.

As to their audience, Lou Reed just hoped "the fans outnumber the event people. When we played the Cartier it was one thousand journalists. A nightmare come true." John Cale was equally sceptical of the inevitable media interest: "We're going to attract a lot of ambulance chasers, people who want to see us fail."

Sterling Morrison mused about their turbulent history: "It is odd the way the band just sort of dissolved, without any seeming reason. There were no big blow-ups, no angry fights – people just... fell off as it went along. *Lou* just dropped off. It was very strange... and since there never was any great apocalyptic moment where we said, 'Screw it, enough is enough, no more of this', that's made it possible for us to come back, just as casually."

Would the old arguments resurface again? Moe Tucker was in positive mood: "I think we've all grown up a lot, calmed down a bit, so that we're all willing to give a little more. More than we were when we were younger." But Lou Reed had the best one-liner about the fact that they were re-forming: "Does that mean 'reformed' as in: now we're good?"

Would all this lead on further, perhaps to new studio recordings? Maureen Tucker was moderately dismissive, in a let's-see-how-it-goes kind of way: "None of us approached this tour with the idea of a new Velvets career – that's not my idea, either. This was to be a special thing, for us to have fun... for once! And also in a way to give all these people who've been buying our records all this time and paying the rent a chance to finally see us."

So in the summer of 1993, thousands of Velvets' aficionados (of all ages – this was a band who were never unfashion-able) were able to see them live in con-cert. Needless to say, the gigs sold out in seconds, leaving thousands more out in the cold.

The June 1993 tour took in Edinburgh, London, Amsterdam, Rotterdam, Hamburg and Prague, where the group were the honoured guests of Czech President Vaclav Havel. As a student, Havel had smuggled a copy of 'White Light/White Heat' into Czechoslovakia, where taped copies of the album and hand-produced lyric books became sym-bols of free speech and artistic expression among those opposing the oppressive yoke of the USSR. As an indi-cation of just how important the Velvets were considered in Czechoslovakia, one should note that when the country was finally able to make the transition from communism to democracy, that process was nicknamed the 'Velvet Revolution'.

After Prague, the tour resumed in Paris, and moved on to Berlin. The Velvets then played five dates in Italy, supporting U2; they also played a brief (and fairly shambolic) set at Britain's Glastonbury Festival. And then it was all over.

But at least the three Paris shows (at L'Olympia Theater) had been taped (and filmed). The result was a live double CD, produced by Mike Rathke. And for fans who might not otherwise be tempted to buy yet *another* live Velvets album, incentive lay in the inclusion of one new Velvets song, the first for decades: 'Coyote'.

Reviews of the shows had been mixed (and reviews of the album and video would be equally divided); once the emotional impact of seeing the four of them reunited on stage (against all expectations) had subsided, many critics levelled accusations that the whole thing was just too 'showbiz' for comfort. The

primary target was Lou Reed – and it's true that vocally he often sounds mannered to the point of self-parody here. On 'Venus In Furs', 'Some Kinda Love', 'I'll Be Your Mirror', 'Rock 'N' Roll' (its third variant spelling !) and even 'Heroin', he sounds like a lounge singer in a cheesy rock cabaret. Cale and Reed had divided Nico's vocal role between them, Reed taking 'I'll Be Your Mirror' while Cale took the rest (to much better effect). Also on the downside, there's the 'Velvet Nursery Rhyme', Lou Reed's verse introduction to the band, which *just* avoids making the listener wince with embarrassment.

Plus points: dynamite versions of 'All Tomorrow's Parties', 'Hey Mr Rain' and 'Sweet Jane'; a quirkily intriguing 'I'm Waiting For The Man'. You also finally get to hear the words to 'Guess I'm Falling In Love' (which features the line "I've got the fever in my pocket", a quote from Bob Dylan's 'Absolutely Sweet Marie'). And – despite all the brouhaha surrounding Cale's departure just prior to recording the third album – 'Pale Blue

THE VELVET UNDERGROUND: LIVE MCMXCIII

Eyes' sounds as if it was always *meant* to feature that mesmeric viola-playing. And (for once), Reed's world-weary vocal approach fits perfectly; I'd say this is the definitive version, and worth the price of admission on its own.

Throughout, the band are sometimes ragged (though charmingly so, in the main), but – enough of the time – in great form, their rapport often uncanny and their playing occasionally approaching the epic. If there are stars of this show, they're John Cale and Moe Tucker, the sheer *solidity* of whose drumming is astonishing (and a stunning visual spectacle, as the video proves). And, of course, state-of-the-art recording technology makes this a lot more accessible than the previous live albums.

As to 'Coyote'... Reed's laconic tale of 'outsider' desert dogs could be an analogy for the Velvets' own troubled history; it could also easily have fitted on 'Loaded'. With its thunderous bass/drum combination, Morrison's delicate guitar work and Reed's dry observations – if it proves to be their swan song, it'll do.

An abbreviated, single-CD version was also released at the same time (and with the same title, confusingly), catalogue number: Sire/Warner Bros 9362-45465-2. Track listing: 'Venus In Furs'/'Sweet Jane'/'Afterhours'/'All Tomorrow's Parties'/'Some Kinda Love'/'The Gift'/'Rock 'N' Roll'/'I'm Waiting For The Man'/'Heroin'/'Pale Blue Eyes'.

A 90-minute video version was also released, titled *Velvet Redux MCMXCIII* (Warner Music 7599 38363-3). Track listing: 'Venus In Furs'/'White Light White Heat'/'Beginning To See The Light'/'Some Kinda Love'/'Femme Fatale'/'Hey Mr. Rain'/'I'm Sticking With You'/'I Heard Her Call My Name'/'I'll Be Your Mirror'/'Rock 'N' Roll'/'Sweet Jane'/'I'm Waiting For The Man'/'Heroin'/'Pale Blue Eyes'/'Coyote'.

PEEL SLOWLY AND SEE

(POLYDOR 31452 7887-2 ; RELEASED ? 1995).

John Cale, 1993: "Now that we've been pleasantly surprised to find that (work and having fun) can co-exist, I think we can get on with a lot more work. I hope we do. That was really the premise under which I really participated in this, and I hope it's borne out."

But behind the scenes, all was not well. Throughout the '93 tour, Lou Reed had distanced himself from the others, to the point where it seemed that he regarded them as just the latest in a long series of backing bands.

Hopes that there would be more concerts to satisfy the thousands who didn't get to see the European dates, perhaps even a new studio album, were dashed in November 1993, when plans for a proposed US tour fell apart in a flurry of "fax fights" between Reed and the others. Though Cale – who had learnt how to pacify Reed during their work on 'Drella' – had played peacemaker during the tour, Reed's attitude to a proposed MTV *Unplugged* show had the duo clashing yet again, this time over "production issues".

Lou Reed: "I said I could no longer continue doing it unless I did the production for any records that were going to come out of it. John Cale didn't want to do that, so that was the end of it."

John Cale: "The idea of handing the reins of The Velvet Underground sound to Lou was like putting the fox in to guard the chicken house, which became a problem when I realised the partnership idea was no longer in existence."

And that was that, again. The official statement from Reed's manager (and ex-wife) Sylvia Reed stated that: "Lou feels he accomplished what he set out to do with the European shows... That being done, he intends to return to his solo work."

Ironically, their public profile had probably never been higher, a measure of which came in December 1993, when

Britain's Channel 4 TV screened an eight-hour-long tribute to the Velvets and Andy Warhol. Official viewing figures showed an audience of 400,000 (not bad, bearing in mind that the show was broadcast in the wee small hours of a Sunday morning).

In 1994 Morrison, Cale and Tucker reunited to perform live as a trio at Pittsburgh's Andy Warhol Museum, playing improvised soundtracks for his Warhol's films 'Eat' and 'Kiss'. They also recorded demos for a possible album project, and there was talk of them taking the Warhol soundtrack show on a European tour in late 1995.

But it wasn't to be. On August 30, 1995, the day after his 53rd birthday, Sterling Morrison died, after a long battle against cancer (non-Hodgkin's lymphoma). How long he'd been ill is unknown (though he doesn't look that well in the *Velvet Redux* video, and in the sleeve notes to the live album Reed refers to Morrison's "courage"). Morrison chose to spend his last weeks at home in Poughkeepsie, New York, and

was visited there by Cale, Tucker ... *and* Reed (who would later write a moving account of his visit for the *New York Times* magazine, titled 'Velvet Warrior').

Understandably, the others were devastated by Morrison's passing. Perhaps none more so than Moe Tucker, who had been closest to him: "I'm heartbroken. I've known him since I was eleven. He was more like a brother than a cohort."

Lou Reed was also stunned, finding it "very, very difficult to accept and believe." He would talk often to the press about Morrison, describing his fellow guitarist's musicianship in glowing terms: "He was in it for music. He wasn't in it for showboating. Sterl was a really great mind, who happened to play guitar."

Reed's 1996 solo album 'Set The Twilight Reeling' would contain an intimations-of-mortality song, 'Finish Line' dedicated "for Sterl".

He also stated, with the same sense of disbelief: "No one will ever hear the four of us play again. That's really sunk in: The Velvet Underground cannot exist." But they still did. In January 1996,

The Velvet Underground were inducted into the Rock And Roll Hall Of Fame. Reed, Cale and Tucker all attended the award ceremony, and performed a new song about Morrison written only two days previously: 'Last Night I Said Goodbye To My Friend'.

Whether Morrison's history of the band was ever finished, and whether the surviving trio will ever record together again are questions only time will answer. It's unlikely that they'd re-recruit Doug Yule, but stranger things have happened in the course of this story.

With timely irony, the Velvets retrospective boxed set was finally released just weeks after Sterling Morrison's death. 'Peel Slowly And See' amply fulfils its purpose (to corral their history, and stem the tide of bootlegs), containing five CDs (their first four albums, re-edited/mixed where necessary, plus a wealth of unreleased material). The packaging echoed that of their first album, complete with (peelable) banana, and the box also contained a well-designed booklet containing an excellent career overview by David Fricke. Much of the archive material had been supplied by Morrison. As an epitaph, one couldn't ask for better.

DISC ONE

Consists of previously unreleased material from John Cale's archives. All are early demo versions recorded at Cale's Ludlow Street apartment in New York during July 1965; Reed and Morrison play guitars, while Cale plays viola and sarinda (an Afghani stringed instrument). There is no drummer, since Angus MacLise had forgotten to turn up for the session. John Cale: "Angus was really living on the Angus calendar. If you told Angus that there was a rehearsal at two o'clock on Friday, he wouldn't understand what you were talking about. He would just come and go, whenever and wherever he pleased."

Though definitely interesting, one doubts if many listeners will return to this disc too often after their initial curiosity has been satisfied. The overall effect is pretty tortuous, partly because there are multiple takes of most of the songs. According to Sterling Morrison, this was because "a lot of the early stuff was conceived in a way that was a lot more laid back than it later became. We were really practising the songs at the same time we were laying them down. 'Okay, that sounds alright. Let's do it again this other way'."

John Cale: "One of the things that we didn't notice at the time but realised later was how very important those early rehearsals were – the way we bummed around on Friday nights and just played and played and played. We started detuning instruments, playing with gadgets, puttering about in general until we landed with something. We spent so much time looking for other ways of doing things. What Lou was singing about was not what rock'n'roll is generally about. Yet there was no reason why this other hybrid could not exist. We were all of a single mind about that."

VENUS IN FURS

Sung by Cale as a folksy ballad, almost in medieval minstrel mode, and sounding somewhere between 'Scarborough Fair' and 'Greensleeves'. It's surprising, given how much Cale hated folk music; and given what the song ultimately became, you find yourself thinking, 'Is this a joke?' Several takes, which pretty much all run together without a break (over fifteen minutes' worth).

PROMINENT MEN

Written by Cale/Reed. Reed sings this Dylanesque protest song (complete with harmonica), railing against the high and mighty. Fairly unremarkable stuff, and it doesn't really fit with the other material, which is probably why it didn't survive in their repertoire.

HEROIN

Reed's wavering voice still sounds ultra-nasal and Dylannish here; but otherwise the bones of the song are all already present in this version, from the arrangement to the pacing. Five takes of this, not all of which make it all the way through (over thirteen minutes' worth).

I'M WAITING FOR THE MAN

Done as a ragtimish country-blues, complete with slide guitar and a bizarre vocal interjection by Cale (stuttering). Three takes of this, with harmonica and viola both painfully messy (just under ten minutes' worth).

WRAP YOUR TROUBLES IN DREAMS

Written by Reed. Sung by Cale as a mournful folk dirge. The metronomic percussion here is provided by Sterling Morrison rapping his knuckles against the back of Cale's sarinda. The song would later be recorded by Nico, on her 'Chelsea Girl' album. Several takes (nearly sixteen minutes' worth), and a brief argument which is a lot more interesting than the music.

ALL TOMORROW'S PARTIES

Done as a folksy ballad, with Cale and Reed harmonising. The first version is really fast, but collapses in a shower of Anglo-Saxon. Eight more (mainly incomplete) takes follow, with varying degrees of success (over eighteen minutes' worth). The most interesting aspect here is that this was recorded nearly six months before they met Warhol.

DISC TWO

Consists of 'The Velvet Underground & Nico' in its entirety, plus the following extra tracks :

ALL TOMORROW'S PARTIES

Mono single version, originally released (as Verve VK 10427) in July 1966. A severe edit of the album version (cut from 5 min. 58 secs. down to 2 min. 49 secs.).

MELODY LAUGHTER

Previously unreleased. Recorded live at the Valleydale Ballroom, Columbus, Ohio on 4/11/66. Writing credited to all four Velvets, plus Nico. Edited down to just under eleven minutes (from thirty). Nico sings, wordlessly. Tucker: "I think there weren't any actual lyrics, just warble... That would go anywhere from two minutes to forty-two. It used to drive me crazy, because it started off with a certain beat, and Lou would just do what he wanted, and the next thing you know, John would be doing what he wanted, and I had to stay at the same beat, and you're hearing this definite other beat... Cale would play the viola, put it down and pick up the bass, put it down, and if we had an organ or something, he'd play that. It just went on and on." Obviously an improvisa-tion-piece, it's dronelike and veers between being interesting and just plain self-indulgent; at times it's pretty painful.

IT WAS A PLEASURE THEN

First released on Nico's 1969 solo album 'Chelsea Girl', and written by Nico, Cale and Reed. John Cale: "Nico had the basic idea and we worked it up – I think." In fact, it sounds like it almost certainly developed out of 'Melody Laughter'. Dirgelike and Gothic, a template that Nico would echo for most of her future career. Recorded at Mayfair Sound Studios in New York, April/May 1967. Produced by Tom Wilson, engineered by Gary Kellgren.

CHELSEA GIRLS

Written by Reed/Morrison. A very folksy ballad, commissioned for the Warhol movie of the same name, but completed too late for inclusion in the film. First released on Nico's 'Chelsea Girl' solo album. Recorded at Mayfair Sound Studios in New York, April/May 1967.

Produced by Tom Wilson, engineered by Gary Kellgren. Orchestral arrangement and conducting by Larry Fallon.

Lou Reed : "Everything on it, those strings, that flute, should have defeated it. But the lyrics, Nico's voice... It managed somehow to survive."

The Chelsea in question is New York's Chelsea Hotel on West 23rd Street, which has been home to many young and literary and artistic types down the decades (usually when they were young and struggling). Dylan Thomas, Arthur Miller, Jackson Pollock, Allen Ginsberg, Edith Piaf, Bob Dylan, Leonard Cohen and Janis Joplin have all lived there; Sid Vicious and Nancy Spungen played out the final act of their tawdry tragedy there. Lou Reed's almost-Dylanesque lyric reads like a roll call of Warhol's Factory crowd (and their sexual and narcotic proclivities); among those mentioned are Ondine, Brigid (Berlin, later Polk), Ingrid (Superstar), Mary (Woronov) and Susan (Bottomly, a.k.a. International Velvet). Nico herself briefly lived at the Chelsea, as did Edie Sedgwick.

Note: Nico's 'Chelsea Girl' features three other songs of note: her versions of 'Wrap Your Troubles In Dreams', John Cale's 'Winter Song' and a Reed/Cale composition, 'Little Sister'.

DISC THREE

Consists of 'White Light/White Heat' in its entirety, 'Stephanie Says' and 'Temptation Inside Your Heart' (from 'VU'), and 'Hey Mr. Rain (Version I)' (from 'Another View'), plus the following previously unreleased tracks :

THERE IS NO REASON

A Reed/Cale song, from a demo acetate recorded early in 1967 at John Cale's Ludlow Street loft in New York. Reed sings this personal-sounding but unremarkable folksy ballad.

SHELTERED LIFE

Written (and sung) by Reed. Recording details as for 'There Is No Reason'. This is *great*! Psychedelic folk, with downright funny lyrics and a kazoo solo, it sounds like something The Purple Gang (of 'Granny Takes A Trip' fame) might have come up with. Reed would later re-record the song for his 1976 album 'Rock And Roll Heart'.

version later recorded for 'White Light/White Heat', and some very weird echoing viola. Sung by Reed in Dylan mode.

IT'S ALL RIGHT (THE WAY THAT YOU LIVE)

Written by Reed/Cale, sung by Reed. Recording details as for 'There Is No Reason'. Somewhere between folk and R&B, it sounds like a B-side, albeit a very good one. A great booming bass line.

I'M NOT TOO SORRY (NOW THAT YOU'RE GONE)

Written by Reed/Cale, sung by Reed. Recording details as for 'There Is No Reason'. Minor folk/pop, overlaid with a lot of psychedelic guitar work.

HERE SHE COMES NOW

Written by Reed/Cale/Morrison. Recording details as for 'There Is No Reason'. With different lyrics to the

GUESS I'M FALLING IN LOVE

Recorded live at the Gymnasium in New York, April 1967. Written by all four Velvets. Good sound quality, and a high energy performance that pisses all over the one on the 1993 live album *and* the instrumental one on 'Another View'.

BOOKER T

Also recorded live at the Gymnasium in New York, April 1967, but here they're fairly sloppy. An instrumental credited to all four Velvets. A three-minute extract from this (six-and-a-half-minute version) was released in 1992 on John Cale's solo album 'Paris S'Eveille'. As mentioned earlier, this track was so-titled because of the inspiration of Booker T & The MG's 'Green Onions'; this would evolve into the backing music for 'The Gift'.

DISC FOUR

Consists of the 'closet mix' of 'The Velvet Underground' album in its entirety, plus 'Foggy Notion', 'I Can't Stand It', 'I'm Sticking With You', 'One Of These Days' and 'Lisa Says' (from 'VU'), plus the following previously unreleased tracks :

WHAT GOES ON

Recorded live 2/10/68 at La Cave, Cleveland, Ohio. A fairly undistinguished live version, with pretty rough sound quality. The point of interest here lies in the fact that it's from Doug Yule's concert début with the band.

IT'S JUST TOO MUCH

From the same era as '1969: Velvet Underground Live', but a different version. This one was recorded live 28/10/69 at The End of Cole Ave, Dallas, Texas. Country blues, but pretty dull.

COUNTESS FROM HONG KONG

Demo version of a song co-written by Cale and Reed, but not recorded until late 1969 (i.e. long after Cale's departure). No other recording details known. With Reed on harmonica, which doesn't seem to fit well; this sounds disturbingly more like bossa nova than folk. It takes its title from Charlie Chaplin's last film as a director; a romantic comedy that starred Sophia Loren and Marlon Brando, it was released in 1967. Lou Reed is evidently a big Chaplin fan – check out 'City Lights' on 'The Bells'.

DISC FIVE

Consists of 'Loaded' in its entirety, but with full-length versions of 'Sweet Jane' and 'New Age' replacing the edited ones from the original release. 'Sweet Jane' gains Reed's intended ending; 'New Age' has an extended closing refrain.

Also included here are a live version of 'I'll Be Your Mirror' (from 'Live At Max's Kansas City'), and the following previously unreleased tracks :

SATELLITE OF LOVE

Out-take from 'Loaded'. Reed would revive the song (with slightly different lyrics) for his 'Transformer' solo album. Here it's still poppy, but not as downright commercial as the Bowie/Ronson arrangement. The subject matter is the painfully promiscuous infidelity of one's partner.

Lou Reed: "That song is about the worst kind of jealousy. You ever been jealous? It's a destructive, horrible emotion. I remember once singing that song on stage and, for some reason, I was suddenly struck so hard by what it was really about. It stopped me in my tracks for an instant, just how intense that kind of jealousy was that I was talking about... I'm just glad the melody was pretty."

WALK AND TALK

Out-take from 'Loaded'. Fairly pedestrian folk/blues sung by Reed, who would re-record it for his first solo album.

OH GIN

Out-take from 'Loaded'. A minor blues, which Reed would re-work (to even lesser effect) as 'Oh Jim' for his solo album 'Berlin'.

SAD SONG

Out-take from 'Loaded'. Achingly beautiful song about a rocky relationship. By the time Reed re-recorded it for 'Berlin' it had become a fairly bitter song about divorce.

OCEAN

Out-take from 'Loaded', which reveals something previously unsuspected – that John Cale had returned to the fold in 1970. "I was brought in by Steve Sesnick in a half-hearted attempt at re-uniting old comrades," Cale explained to David Fricke. This version is more moodily melodramatic vocally than that from the 'lost' album included on 'VU', but features some great guitar work and Cale's atmospheric organ-playing swells like a

tide ; Reed would re-record the song yet
again for his eponymous début album
in 1972.

RIDE INTO THE SUN
Out-take from 'Loaded', and another
re-recording of a song from the 'lost'
album. The version on 'Another View'
was an instrumental; this time it has
words that reveal it as a wish for escape
(and it *still* sounds very Beatle-inflenced).
Written byReed/Cale/Tucker/Morrison ;
also re-recorded by Reed for his first
solo album.

SOME KINDA LOVE
Laconically bluesy live version; an out-take
from 'Live At Max's Kansas City'.

I LOVE YOU
Out-take from 'Loaded'. As the title
implies, a straightforward love song from
Reed; sadly, it isn't a very good one.

ANTHOLOGIES

There have been numerous 'best of' compilations down the years, most of them recycling the same (obvious) selection of material without much care or attention. An exception, and thus the best of the bunch, is:

THE BEST OF THE VELVET
UNDERGROUND
(WORDS AND MUSIC OF LOU REED)
(VERVE/POLYGRAM 841 164; RELEASED 1989)

'I'm Waiting For The Man'/'Femme Fatale'/ 'Run, Run, Run'/'Heroin'/'All Tomorrow's Parties'/'I'll Be Your Mirror'/'White Light/ White Heat'/'Stephanie Says'/'What Goes On'/'Beginning To See The Light'/'Pale Blue Eyes'/'I Can't Stand It'/'Lisa Says'/ 'Sweet Jane'/'Rock 'N' Roll'.

Decent sound quality, and an intelligent (if slightly lopsided) overview. But then, the Velvets' output isn't really in need of abbreviation, is it?

INDEX

AFTER HOURS	32
ALL TOMORROW'S PARTIES	9, 91, 92
ANDY'S CHEST	56
BEGINNING TO SEE THE LIGHT	31
BOOKER T	94
CANDY SAYS	29
CHELSEA GIRLS	92
CONEY ISLAND STEEPLECHASE	62
COOL IT DOWN	41
COUNTESS FROM HONG KONG	95
EUROPEAN SON	12
FEMME FATALE	7
FERRYBOAT BILL	63
FOGGY NOTION	55
GUESS I'M FALLING IN LOVE (INSTRUMENTAL VERSION)	63, 94
HEAD HELD HIGH	41
HERE SHE COMES NOW	22
HEROIN	10, 91
HEY MR. RAIN (VERSION I)	62
HEY MR. RAIN (VERSION II)	63
I CAN'T STAND IT	53
I FOUND A REASON	42
I HEARD HER CALL MY NAME	22
I LOVE YOU	97

I'LL BE YOUR MIRROR 11
I'M GONNA MOVE RIGHT IN 62
I'M NOT TOO SORRY (NOW THAT YOU'RE GONE) 94
I'M SET FREE 31
I'M STICKING WITH YOU 59
I'M WAITING FOR THE MAN 6, 91
IT WAS A PLEASURE THEN 92
IT'S ALL RIGHT (THE WAY THAT YOU LIVE) 94
IT'S JUST TOO MUCH 95
JESUS 31
LADY GODIVA'S OPERATION 20
LISA SAYS 55
LONESOME COWBOY BILL 42
MELODY LAUGHTER 92
NEW AGE 41
OCEAN 55, 96
OH GIN 96
OH! SWEET NUTHIN' 42
ONE OF THESE DAYS 56
PALE BLUE EYES 30
PROMINENT MEN 91
RIDE INTO THE SUN 62, 97
ROCK & ROLL 40
ROCK AND ROLL 63
RUN RUN RUN 9

SAD SONG 96
SATELLITE OF LOVE 96
SHE'S MY BEST FRIEND 55
SHELTERED LIFE 93
SISTER RAY 22
SOME KINDA LOVE 30, 97
STEPHANIE SAYS 53
SUNDAY MORNING 6
SWEET JANE 40
TEMPTATION INSIDE YOUR HEART 56
THAT'S THE STORY OF MY LIFE 31
THE BLACK ANGEL'S DEATH SONG 11
THE GIFT 20
THE MURDER MYSTERY 32
THERE IS NO REASON 93
THERE SHE GOES AGAIN 11
TRAIN AROUND THE BEND 42
VENUS IN FURS 8, 90
WALK AND TALK 96
WE'RE GONNA HAVE A REAL GOOD TIME TOGETHER 62
WHAT GOES ON 29, 95
WHITE LIGHT/WHITE HEAT 19
WHO LOVES THE SUN 40
WRAP YOUR TROUBLES IN DREAMS 91

SONGS FOR DRELLA - A FICTION

A DREAM	79
FACES AND NAMES	77
FOREVER CHANGED	79
HELLO, IT'S ME	79
I BELIEVE	78
IMAGES	77
IT WASN'T ME	77
NOBODY BUT YOU	78
OPEN HOUSE	76
SLIP AWAY (A WARNING)	77
SMALLTOWN	76
STARLIGHT	76
STYLE IT TAKES	76
TROUBLE WITH CLASSICISTS	76
WORK	76